CREATURES FROM THE CALDERA

A.E. PILLOW

THE WHUMPY PRINTING PRESS

Cover Illustration by Hen Towers

Cover Design by Nicole Alessi

To my mom and sisters

CONTENTS

CONTENT WARNINGS

This story contains the following content:

- Animal attacks

- Character death

- Whipping

- Broken bones

- Cave-ins

If this book isn't for you, no worries! But if it is, we hope you enjoy this story about some misfit guards and some very unfriendly cats ...

1

THE UNUSUAL

Ivy climbed to the top of the watchtower shortly after sunset, throwing her day pack on the floor of the small wooden structure with a grunt.

"Fucking tower duty," she mumbled. For the most part, Ivy liked being stationed as a guard on the Caldera. The population was sparse, the wilderness vast. She would much rather be out in the wilderness, though, not stuck in a tower watching for non-existent threats.

Ivy sat and looked out at the thick pine forest and the rim of the Caldera rising above it. The slope was gentle at first but turned into a sheer rock cliff for the last hundred feet or so. It was impossible to get over and into the Caldera. It did lend a bit of spookiness to the area, Ivy supposed.

"Nothing out there," she said. Nothing had come out of the Caldera ... ever. Children's tales. The three guard stations on the rim, the guard towers, the fort below, were all just there to get rid of subpar members of the guard, the weird ones that no one knew what else to do with. Again, Ivy quite liked that most of the time, but she had a realistic view of what duty on the Caldera was.

The trees below were bathed in shadows and the moon was just rising when Ivy decided she was going to sleep. She wasn't supposed to, of course, but who was going to catch her?

As she moved to the back of the wooden tower, the ground shook beneath her, sending her sprawling on the floor. Something snapped beneath her, and the hut pitched to the side.

"The fuck ... " Ivy got up carefully, the lantern she had brought with her somehow still lit. She looked around, listened. As her pounding heart started to calm, her mind caught up to what had happened.

Earthquake.

A decently big one at that. Ivy was used to tremors, but it had been years since one so large had hit.

Well, at least she was going to be able to get off tower duty. She should get back to the station and report the damage. First she had to get out of the fucking tower before it collapsed and killed her. She moved slowly toward the door, which was now pitched toward the ground. She was surprised it hadn't been knocked open. Ivy took a deep breath and scooted on the floor to the door and got outside onto the little wraparound porch. She tried to ignore the way her arms were shaking. She looked down at the ladder, and it seemed to be intact to a point just above the ground, easy enough for her to jump off.

Ivy thought she heard something and glanced at the forest and the Caldera beyond. She squinted. Something felt a little off, but she couldn't figure out what it was.

She shimmied along to the ladder and started down. The gap between the bottom and the ground was a bit larger than she thought, but the base of the tower was mostly grass, so she took a chance. She tucked and rolled and got off with no more than a minor cut on her arm. Probably didn't even need stitches.

Ivy adjusted her pack and took off to East Station. It would only take a quarter hour or so if she walked quickly, and she would do so in the chilly autumn air.

She'd only been walking for a few minutes when thick fog rolled in through the trees. There was a strange smell to it, not a smell she would associate with any volcanic activity. It smelled like ... sweet rot? Like apples that had fallen off a tree and had been on the ground quite some time. Ivy tried to ignore the smell and the fog, but it was odd. She'd been at the Caldera her whole adult life and had never seen fog that thick, and the smell was bothersome. She knew there were no apple trees around that part of the forest.

"Focus," she told herself. It was just fog. Normal fog. It was just an earthquake, just fog, there was nothing abnormal about anything going on, or at least not dangerously abnormal.

At last, she saw the lights of the station ahead.

Something darted across the path before her and Ivy blinked.

"What the fuck."

Ivy had been roaming around the Caldera for over twenty years and had never, ever seen anything like what just ran before her. It was perhaps the size of a bobcat but much too slender and, well, it might have been a trick of the light, but it looked green and somehow shiny in the moonlight. Something about it made Ivy want to run.

She walked as calmly as she could toward the station. If there was something predatory out there, it would chase her if she ran. She was almost at the station, and once she got in, she would be safe.

Someone screamed from inside the station. At nearly the same time, something growled behind her, a sound not unlike a house cat growling. Ivy drew her sword, or tried to, but something hit her from behind, landing on her pack, knocking her off balance, and sending her sprawling face-first into the grass.

Something was ripping and tearing, luckily just into her pack, giving Ivy a moment to regain her composure. She rolled over and drew her knife from her belt. The creature skittered away for a moment then jumped toward her chest. She managed to dodge, and the creature's claws tore into her arm.

Ivy grunted in pain and took a stab at the creature. She wasn't sure if it was a fatal hit, but the creature ran away. There were more screams from the station.

"Fuck!" Her arm was bleeding badly. She slipped off the path and into the forest for enough time to pull her med kit out of her backpack and quickly wrap the arm. She stood and immediately stumbled back against the tree.

There were more of them. A lot more. At least five creatures were staring at her, hissing and growling. Ivy knew she wasn't going to be able to deal with them all. There were more screams coming from the station.

One of the creatures jumped for her, and Ivy tried to hit it but slipped on the dewy grass and tumbled down the hill. She landed with a splash in the pond below. She looked out into the moonlit night and waited for the creatures to attack.

"Where are you, little fuckers."

They weren't coming. Did they not like water? Ivy started to shiver, but she thought maybe she should stay put for a little bit.

By the sound of the screams from the station, there was nothing she could do there.

***

Calla made her way up to the roof of the fort to look for the station lights. She paced back and forth while she waited. Most nights she was there at midnight on the dot, stood still, saw the lights, and went back to her room. It was, on a normal night, a ten-minute routine.

Tonight was different.

Earlier that evening, an earthquake shook the area, and Calla had a bad feeling that one of the stations wouldn't light. Everyone else had gone to bed as usual, sure that things were fine, but Calla knew something was wrong. Something bad happened hours ago, and she was going to be the one to see it. It was up to her to see it.

West Station lit up first, then, shortly after it, Mid Station. Calla looked to where she knew the light for East Station would be.

Nothing. No light. Calla looked at the other stations again and back to East Station. Still there was no light. Calla knew there was something wrong, but she waited a few more minutes just to be sure then went down and straight to Captain Marcus.

"Something wrong, Calla?"

Calla jumped. "Damn you, Zero." Zero laughed, standing up from where he had been crouching in the dark near the captain's quarters. He ran his hand through his light hair and, still smiling from scaring her, spoke.

"So, something wrong?"

"East Station didn't light," Calla said. "I need to inform Captain Marcus. I think we should lead a party tonight to see why."

"Always doom and gloom with you, Calla," Zero said.

"And you're never serious, are you? They didn't light for a reason, what if there was a collapse or something and people are hurt?"

"I know. Get your pack and meet me out front in five. Marcus authorized a quick foray in the dark," Zero said.

"Just the two of us?" Calla said.

"For now," Zero said. "Come on, better than nothing, isn't it?"

"Right," Calla said, leaving Zero and heading to her quarters for her pack. While she was worried about East Station, she didn't really fancy going on the journey with Zero and just Zero. The man annoyed her to no end. He annoyed most people and seemed to like doing so. But she didn't really have a choice in the matter, so with Zero she would go.

The night air was chilly but the moon was shining bright. Calla had been up to the stations many times in her years at the fort, but there was always something about going there at night that made it feel like one could get lost.

Zero took the lead, and Calla thought she could at least trust him to not get them lost. She'd rather be going through the dark forest with Ivy, though, an expert navigator, versus the joke of the whole Caldera.

As they wound through the forest and up to the stations, a thick fog set in. Oddly thick. Calla couldn't remember fog that thick before, especially when the weather had been so dry. It gave her an odd feeling. No light, thick fog, earthquake.

Calla had grown up on legends centered around the dangers of the Caldera. Most people discarded them as just stories, things that hadn't happened or were figurative and not to be taken literally. Tales of danger and monsters and brave deeds. There was truth there, Calla always thought, and all the stories were swirling in her head just as the fog was swirling around her and Zero.

Calla hoped it wouldn't take too long to get to the station.

"Bit like a scary story out here tonight, isn't it?" Zero asked.

"Indeed."

"Nervous, Calla?"

"A bit, you're not?"

"A bit, it is rather creepy out tonight. I wouldn't worry too much. We're guards after all, aren't we? We're supposed to be brave, right?"

"I know," Calla said, glad it was too dark for Zero to see her blush. She was being a bit cowardly, she supposed. They continued on through the fog with the moonshine almost making it worse.

Zero, on the other hand, almost seemed happy to be going to the station in the middle of the night.

Calla groaned.

"Yes?"

"You're going to the station because you want to sleep with someone there, aren't you?" Calla said.

"Well, that might be one of the reasons," Zero said with a smile. Calla scoffed, but they were at least going to the station, so she supposed she should be happy with that. She should have realized sooner what Zero was up to; he slept around with quite a few guards. It wasn't hard to see why; he was, by most standards, handsome. Calla could see it even though she never really cared to look at men that way.

Suddenly Zero stopped ahead of her. "Do you smell that?"

"What? No. I don't smell anything."

"It smells like blood," Zero said.

Calla scoffed, "Zero ... "

"No, really. You don't smell that?"

Calla took a deep breath. She couldn't smell anything, or, well, nothing unusual. She looked at Zero. He was standing still and looking around, his hand on the pommel of his sword. It looked like he was serious about it.

"Keep an eye out," he said.

"Yes, sir," Calla said. In all likelihood, the worst it could be was a coyote or some other animal killed nearby. There was danger there, but it was more likely they would scare off the creatures or see them long before they attacked. And Calla didn't even smell anything.

"Fuck," Zero mumbled ahead of her as he stopped. Calla approached and looked down at the ground.

Blood.

A rather large slick of blood in the grass on the path. Zero lifted his lantern and looked side to side. Calla did the same but didn't see anything. She didn't hear anything, didn't smell anything.

"We're almost at the station," Zero said. "Side by side." Calla walked with Zero, knowing that the station was dead ahead and wanting to run to it. They came upon the station, and for just a moment, Calla was relieved. Then she started noticing things.

The station was dark. There was no noise. She could smell the blood. Zero was right, the coppery smell of blood hung heavy in the air, and there were other scents with it that Calla didn't want to think about.

Beside her, Zero drew his sword and she followed suit. The door to the station was ajar and Zero pushed it open. The first body was right inside the door. They both froze. Calla looked around the courtyard, the dim light of the lantern revealing more bodies. Calla clapped a hand over her mouth to keep from screaming. She blinked away tears and tried to keep breathing.

There were a dozen people at each station. Calla counted the bodies she could see, the task the only thing keeping her sane. She looked at Zero and held up nine fingers then drew her finger across her throat; nine dead. So three were missing.

Zero pointed outside then up. Ah, there would be a guard out in the tower, but that left two missing in the station and no sign of what had caused the carnage. Zero moved forward and Calla followed. As they reached each body, it was clear there was no point in checking for life. Around the back they found the last two bodies.

Calla looked down at the closest body. So many of them were mauled beyond recognition, but the body nearest her was not.

Lana. The guard's name was Lana and she had only been there a year. Calla had been the one to give her the orientation tour. Calla knelt and closed Lana's eyes. With her lantern closer to the body, she could see the wounds better. A few years back, a guard had been mauled nearly to death by a bear. Calla had seen the aftermath of the incident, and there was no doubt in her mind that the wounds that killed Lana were made by some sort of animal.

Zero shifted a little and Calla stood.

Eleven dead. No sign of what killed them. Zero led her back out of the station and down the path for a little bit before stopping.

"What the fuck did that?" he asked.

"I don't know. An animal of some sort."

Zero let out a shaky breath and ran a hand through his hair. He took a couple of deep breaths. Calla felt like the world around her couldn't be real.

"Right. We need backup, as quickly as possible. We need to warn the other stations and the fort, but if … if we get taken down, no one will know. Thoughts?"

"This can't be real," Calla said.

A groan interrupted Zero, and both he and Calla jumped. There was something in the forest right off the path. It sounded human to Calla, and there was someone missing … Calla stepped into the forest before Zero could say anything.

There was a body slumped against a pine tree just a few steps off the path. Calla lifted her lantern, expecting to see yet another corpse, but when the light hit the person's face, they looked up at Calla.

"Ivy! Zero, it's Ivy and she's alive."

Ivy's left arm was bleeding; she'd wrapped a bandage around it. Calla looked for any other wounds, sure that there must be something else keeping the woman on the ground. Ivy was soaking wet and shivering.

"Ivy?"

Ivy moaned and her hand twitched.

"What do we have, Calla?"

"Wounded arm and it looks like she fell into the pond, she's shivering," Calla said.

"We need to get her out of here," Zero said.

"Ivy, can you get up and walk?" Calla asked.

"Can try," Ivy replied.

"Good, we'll help you get back to the fort," Zero said.

"Station?"

"All lost," Zero said. Ivy grunted. They managed to get Ivy on her feet, and she could stand a little. It was going to be an awkward trip down to the fort; Ivy and Zero were both quite a bit taller than Calla.

It took a little bit to get a rhythm going, but once they did, they started making good time down the hill back toward the fort. As they went, Ivy regained some of her strength and was able to move better.

"Do you smell that?" Zero asked. "Smells like apples."

"Fuck, that's them," Ivy said. "Keep going."

"Did you see them?" Calla asked.

"Smaller than a bobcat, skinny. Green," Ivy said.

Calla could have done with a little more description, but that was good enough for the moment. Once they got Ivy back to the fort and they were all safe, they could talk more in detail.

Once they dipped out of the fog, the smell disappeared and Ivy could walk on her own.

Finally they made it to the fort, and Zero and Calla shut the fort door firmly behind them.

"Right, Calla, can you make sure Ivy gets to the infirmary, stay there with her, I'll get Captain Marcus and meet you two there," Zero said.

"Got it," Calla said.

"I can go there myself," Ivy muttered.

"Just to be sure," Calla said, "then Captain Marcus will know where to find us. I'm sure he'll have questions."

They walked into the infirmary where Ramona was sitting and reading something. She jumped a little as she saw Ivy and Calla.

"Oh goodness, what happened, Ivy?"

"Attacked. Sat in the freezing water too long."

"Well, I can see that, but what did this?"

"I don't know," Ivy said.

Ramona frowned and looked at Calla.

"It was some sort of unknown creature," Calla said, not knowing really what else she could say.

"Just sew me up," Ivy said.

"Working on it," Ramona said. "Let's get you out of these clothes first." Ivy nodded and Ramona led her behind a curtain to change.

Calla settled back and sighed. What a weird night, and it wasn't over yet. What the hell had just happened? What the hell had killed all those at the station? Eleven people were killed by a skinny green cat? How many had there been? Were the other stations in danger?

Calla tried not to worry, but images of the dead kept popping into her mind. The smell of blood. Calla had never seen such carnage. She knew every single one of the people there, and had known many of them for years. She tried not to cry and failed.

"Calla, you alright over there?"

"No, but I don't think there's anything you can do about it," Calla said, wiping away the tears.

"I'm assuming the captain is aware of whatever this is?"

"Yes, he should be here soon," Calla said.

"Can you help me over here, Calla?" Ramona asked.

"Sure," she said. She really didn't want to see blood and injuries, but she wanted to help Ramona with Ivy. It mostly involved holding a light so Ramona could stitch Ivy up. Ivy groaned and cursed and twisted when Ramona would pull away.

"I could hold your hand," Calla said.

"Fuck off, Calla," Ivy said.

"Sorry," Calla muttered. She didn't like touching people without asking first. She didn't like when people did that to her, but maybe Ivy had thought she was teasing or something. Or that was just Ivy. Calla didn't know sometimes. She wished she did, especially with Ivy. Ivy was beautiful. Calla pushed the thought out of her mind. It wasn't the time to think about such things. She really didn't want to think of anything, actually.

Calla wished very much that nothing about the day had gone the way it had, and she couldn't even be glad it was over because she had a feeling it was only the beginning.

2

DAWN

Ivy's arm was throbbing, and she really, really didn't want to have to talk to more than one person. She knew she was going to sound a bit crazy with what she had to report. She was also worried that strange, deadly creatures roaming the hillside would mean she would have to stay in the fort. Or worse, she would have to lead people through the forest in search of the creatures.

Ivy sighed. Ramona was busing herself with cleaning up, and Calla was staring off into space, looking rather dejected. Ivy felt a little bad about snapping at her earlier.

At last, Zero and Captain Marcus came in. Both looked tired and annoyed. Good. If Ivy had to be annoyed, everyone else should too.

"What Zero's just told me sounds like a bunch of madness," Captain Marcus said. "I'm in no mood for madness. I can see Ivy is hurt, so that's the truth. Calla, what did you find at the station?"

"The bodies of eleven guards," Calla said.

"Elaborate."

"The bodies were torn and bloody, the lights were out at the station, there was no sign of what had attacked."

"You're sure the bodies were dead?"

"Yes, sir."

"Have you ever seen a dead body before, Calla?"

"Yes, but not so brutally killed."

"Then how were you sure they were dead?"

"No movement, no breathing, the smell ... There's no mistaking it, they're dead."

"Hmm. Ivy, how were you injured?"

"I was attacked by some sort of creature, sir."

"You didn't get a good look?"

"It was smaller than a bobcat and looked feline a bit, but it was longer and slender. It was green."

"Why were you outside the station and why didn't you help those inside?"

"I was on tower duty. The earthquake damaged the tower so much it's unsafe. I was on my way to report it when I was attacked. I was able to get away from the first creature, but then five more showed up. I fell down the hill into a pond, and for some reason, they didn't attack me. I waited for them to leave, then I headed up the hill and ran into Zero and Calla."

"Ramona, do you know what caused the wounds you just sewed up?"

"Animal, but unlike any I've ever seen," Ramona said.

Marcus sighed and looked at the group. "I find this all very difficult to believe."

"So do we, sir," Ivy said. As fucking weird as it was, denying belief in the face of all the evidence was stupid, and she felt like saying just that to the captain.

"Sir, we just lost an entire station, we have to check in with the others," Zero cut in before Marcus could speak.

"Right. One last thing before we move on. If this is a prank or some sort of cover up, that's it for you three." Marcus indicated Ivy, Calla, and Zero. "Ivy and Calla, you'll be expelled from the guard, and you, Zero, you'll be tried and I will push for execution."

"Understood," Zero said.

"Right. I'm taking a squad to East Station; until then, you three need to stay here. Once I return and find out what's going on, I'll deal with you," Marcus said, leaving the room in a huff.

"That went well," Ivy said.

"Are ... are they really all dead?" Ramona asked.

"Yes," Zero said. "I'm sorry."

"Do you think the others really are in danger?" Ramona asked.

"I don't know," Zero said. "Who knows how many of those things there are. How much do they eat when they hunt, were they even hunting? We don't know a damn thing."

"Seems like there was a danger in the Caldera after all," Ivy said.

Zero was pacing back and forth and frowning. It would almost be comical if things weren't so dire.

Calla frowned. "What are you thinking?"

"That we really need to go warn the other stations. Marcus didn't believe us, though I don't fully blame him. This is insane, but we know better, and I don't think we should risk lives for want of proof."

"Marcus was very clear what the repercussions would be," Calla said.

"If we were lying, which we're not," Zero said.

"I love it here, but I could survive expulsion from the guard. Zero, he threatened to have you killed," Calla said.

"I know, but I think it's worth the risk," Zero said. "Will you come with me?"

"Not an order?"

"No. This is potentially dangerous and possibly seditious. I could use the help, but this is volunteer only."

"I'm going," Calla said.

"So am I."

Calla and Zero turned to look at Ivy. She knew she looked like shit and that maybe it was safer to stay where she was, but she also knew she wasn't fucking crazy and wanted proof of that.

"You're up to it?" Zero asked.

"Yes, and it makes sense, I'm the only one that's seen one of the things. And if we have to go off the path, I can get us safely home better than anyone here," Ivy said. "Also it pisses me off that Marcus didn't believe us even though I almost had my fucking arm ripped off."

"That's good enough for me. Let's move out," Zero said. Ivy sighed and hoped she was making the right decision.

***

For the second time that night, Calla found herself leaving the fort in the dark. It still didn't quite feel real. If both stations were safe and well, they might be able to take a bit of a rest. If they weren't thrown in a cell when Marcus caught up with them.

"So, these things are small, green, cat-like creatures with claws. Did they make any sounds?" Zero asked.

"Hissing, it sounded like a pissed off house cat," Ivy said, "and there were a lot of them, but they were hard to see even with the moonlight."

"And they smell like rotting apples," Zero said. "That gives them away a bit."

"I just can't work out why they killed all those people in East Station but didn't eat them," Calla said.

"Maybe they like their meat a bit putrid," Ivy said.

"That's disturbing, but possibly true," Zero said.

"I'm glad we're not headed there," Calla said. "I don't want to see that again." She hoped that the other stations were alright. The images she saw earlier that night were starting to wind into her mind. She'd known all the guards who'd been killed.

The country was not at war and hadn't been for a few hundred years. Calla had grown up in a small town where there wasn't much violence. She'd lost family over the years, of course, but none of them violently. Prior to that night, the worst violence she had seen was a fellow guard who had taken a bad fall and broken several bones and had deep gashes. Now she'd seen eleven dead, torn into pieces. She didn't think she would ever forget the smell of blood and guts and excrement.

Calla took a deep breath.

"You're doing great, Calla," Zero said quietly. "Thank you for coming with me."

"Of course. I don't want anyone else to get hurt."

"Once we're sure everyone is warned, if you need to go off and cry or scream or break down in any way, let me know."

"I will," she said.

"Gonna let me cry too?" Ivy cut in.

"Of course, but I don't think you're shy about the whole thing," Zero said. "I'm guessing you'll take your anger and grief out by killing some of these beasts. Or hell, I could be wrong, and Calla will go for slaughter and you'll break down crying."

Ivy snorted. "Slaughter sounds about right for me."

"And what about you, Zero, crying or killing?" Calla asked.

"I'll start with making sure no one else is hurt, then we'll see," Zero said.

Calla hoped that she could shove the feelings aside to wait for a good time to break down. She knew emotion was one of the reasons she was stationed at the Caldera. It made sense that they would put her here where they didn't expect there to be any danger. She didn't blame them, and she desperately hoped she wouldn't embarrass herself.

Most of the people who were stationed at the Caldera were odd. Ivy certainly was. She was brash and kept to herself and didn't want to be around people for the most part. There was something about her, though, that made Calla wish she could spend more time with Ivy. Well, she was getting to spend a bit of time with her now, but the situation was less than ideal. As for why Zero was at the Caldera, Calla wasn't sure. There were a lot of nasty rumors about him. Calla supposed they really didn't matter as far as the present situation was concerned.

They made it to Middle Station in under an hour, and Calla felt nervous as they approached. It was quiet, but it was the wee hours of the morning. There was also light and no smell of blood or rotting apples.

As they approached the door, someone inside opened it, looking half asleep and confused.

"Lieutenant Zero?"

"Yes, I ... "

"What are you doing here?" The door opened further to reveal Captain Marcus, arms folded across his chest.

"We really thought ... "

"Silence. I don't actually want to hear whatever excuse you've got, not after what you've done."

"Sir?" Zero frowned and stiffened.

"What did you do at East Station and where are the bodies?" Marcus asked.

"What ... I didn't ... the creatures ... " Zero looked back at Calla and Ivy.

"Get in here, you three," Marcus said, and they all three filed in. Zero looked at Calla again, and she gave a shrug. She had no idea what could be going on. What did Marcus mean, there were no bodies? How could that be?

"Sir ... "

"Silence, Calla, you still have a chance to save your life. That goes for you as well, Ivy. Lieutenant Hana, please escort Zero here to a cell. Calla and Ivy, you go to the main hall and wait for me," Marcus said.

They made their way to the hall, and Calla sat down in a daze with Ivy across from her. She wondered if she was going crazy. How could the bodies be gone? She had seen them with her own eyes. Why did Marcus think Zero had anything to do with what was going on?

"Calla?"

"Sorry, what was that?"

"Things are fucked," Ivy said.

"Very."

Ivy sighed. "I'm leaving."

"What?"

"I'm going to West Station to warn them. Someone fucking has to and I think you'll do a better job than me of keeping Marcus from killing Zero."

"Fuck," Calla said.

Ivy snorted a laugh. "Fuck indeed, but are we on the same page here? Those fucking things are real. West Station needs to be warned and someone has to protect Zero."

"I didn't think you liked him."

"I didn't think you did either," Ivy said.

Calla shrugged. "He's annoying when nothing is going on, but tonight ... "

"An actual calm leader, who'd have thought?"

"I'll do the best I can to protect him. Be safe, Ivy," Calla said.

"I will," Ivy said. Calla sighed and put her head in her hands. This was all getting so wildly out of hand. She didn't understand why Marcus was being the way he was. People had died! They should be regrouping at the fort and figuring out what to do next! It was impossible to say how many of the creatures there were, but there were a limited number of guards to deal with them and they had already lost nearly a dozen.

"Calla." She jumped slightly as Captain Marcus entered. "Where is Ivy?"

"She went to the bathroom," Calla said. Marcus was going to be furious when he realized Ivy wasn't there, and Calla hoped she was far enough away by then. Of course, it was Ivy, and she knew the forest better than anyone and could easily evade anyone sent after her.

"Right. I want to talk to you alone, anyway. Calla, this is a serious offense."

"Sir, I'm sorry, I'm confused. What do you think happened? Zero was at the fort all evening until I saw East Station fail to light. Then he and I found the dead and rescued Ivy."

"No one saw Zero for several hours in the evening. He had time to go to the station and back," Marcus said.

"You really think he killed guards? What of Ivy?"

"I'm worried she helped. I wish I could have seen her wounds before they were sewn."

"I'm sorry, sir, that just doesn't make any sense."

"Doesn't it? I've seen guards go mad here. Ivy has never fit in, she dislikes most people. Zero has history," Marcus said. "They got bored, went to East Station, and slaughtered everyone there. Then Zero volunteered to go check things out with you, knowing you'd be easy to fool, especially with an injured Ivy lying in wait."

Calla couldn't help the blush that spread across her cheeks. Easy to fool. Was she? Ivy wasn't very social, but Calla really didn't think she would go off and kill people out of boredom. And Zero ...

"Zero's history?"

Marcus sighed. "Zero was stationed in the south for his first few years on the guard. He was on a training mission and his entire squad was killed. Poisoned. Zero claimed that they all drank from the same tainted water. He claimed to have almost died himself, but there was no proof. They couldn't charge him and moved him here."

Calla had to admit it was rather odd, but still, she couldn't see why Zero, or Ivy for that matter, would want to kill people. Ivy's wounds had looked like an animal had made them. The guards looked like they had been torn apart. How had Zero killed them all and gotten no wounds?

"The bodies were torn apart, quite different from poison."

"Unless he did the cutting once the guards were incapacitated."

"That doesn't seem likely. I'm sorry, sir, I don't think Zero or Ivy did this."

"Green cats did?"

"Yes," Calla said. "I know it seems crazy, but I believe it was creatures more than Zero and Ivy. That just doesn't make sense to me."

"Calla, you're risking expulsion or worse," Marcus said.

"I know."

Marcus sighed. Just as he was about to speak, one of his men walked in and whispered something in his ear.

"Ivy is gone," Marcus said.

"She is?" Calla frowned.

Marcus shook his head. "That's why they wanted you. Naive. A fool. Too stuck in stories to see what is really going on."

Calla knew she was right. She knew Zero hadn't killed anyone. She knew Ivy was telling the truth about the creatures. There were just too many signs that the creatures were there. Calla didn't know what she could say or how she could say it to get Marcus to believe her.

Calla started crying.

"You help me, side with me, and I can protect you, Calla. You don't have to worry about Zero or Ivy hurting you."

Calla shook her head. "I believe them. There are creatures out there, they are dangerous, and we should be doing something about them."

Marcus sighed and looked over his shoulder. "Lock her up too."

3

A Light in the Dark

Ivy made it out of the station easily. She just walked like she had purpose and no one stopped her. Marcus just thought she'd follow his order. She supposed she should have done it, it was how the chain of command worked after all, but Marcus was an ass and if Ivy stayed, she was going to blow up in his face and get in fucking trouble anyway. Better to let Calla deal with Marcus. Oh, the woman was a bit sensitive, but her heart was in the right place and she could help Zero more than Ivy could.

It was starting to get light as she left the station and headed to West Station. The fog was clearing as the light chased the night away. Ivy paused now and then to listen for any odd sounds and sniff the air for the smell of rotting apples. Nothing seemed off; the morning chorus of birds was starting to sing as usual.

"Fucking Marcus," she said. If the bastard didn't have such a problem with Zero, they could move forward with the fact that strange green cats were fucking killing people.

Ivy knew why Marcus was after Zero, or at least she knew the basics. Zero was the sole survivor of a training mission gone wrong. Everyone thought Zero had something to do with it. A lot of people didn't quite trust Zero, and it was clear that Marcus didn't trust him and more; he seemed to particularly have it out for Zero.

Stupid. The whole fucking thing was stupid.

Ivy picked up the pace as she neared the station. She was tired and would like to take a nap if she could before heading out.

At first all looked well; there were no bodies on display, no groans of pain, nothing on fire. It looked exactly as a station should look in the early morning. She knocked on the side door and waited for the night watch to open it.

Nothing.

She knocked again. Maybe it was guard switch time. Ivy sighed.

"Wake up, fuckers!" she yelled.

Still nothing. Ivy was just considering breaking in the door when the wind picked up a little and a horrible smell reached her. Blood. Shit. Death.

"Oh fuck no," Ivy groaned. She didn't want to see what was in the station, and it seemed likely everyone within was dead, but with fucking Marcus being a dick, she needed proof. Ivy stepped back, positioning herself so she could try to kick the door open. It took a couple of tries, but the door finally opened.The first body was just a few feet away from the door.

Torn open, insides missing. Ivy took a deep breath and moved forward, trying to push it out of her mind that she knew who the body had been. The courtyard had blood and bits of bodies all around. She tried to ignore the fact that her legs were shaking and pushed forward.

"Fuck, fuck, fuck," Ivy muttered as she moved around. She went into the central building and made her way up into the tower to see if she could spot anything useful before she left the fucking place.

There was something odd about a patch of grass outside; it almost looked wet. It was blood. The sun rose above the Caldera and hit the blood, turning it almost golden. Ivy saw patches of blood here and there heading north and then east toward the Caldera, toward …

"The caves. Fuck," Ivy said. She had to get back to Mid Station as fast as she could. Something crashed below her and Ivy jumped. Fuck, the things were still there. Ivy drew her sword as she descended from the tower. She saw movement.

"Ivy?"

Ivy looked at the bloody man before her and tried desperately to remember his name. "Asher?" Two more guards stood behind Asher, bloody as well.

"What … what is going on?" Asher asked.

"The earthquake did something and released these things," Ivy said. "We're working on it. Are you three all that's left here?"

Asher nodded.

"We should get to Mid Station where the others are," Ivy said.

"Your arm," Asher noted, his unspoken question clear.

"East Station got attacked, all gone but me. Mid is alright and so is the fort."

"What the hell is going on," Asher sighed.

"An attack. I ... let's get reorganized as best we can and get out of here," Ivy said. She could tell that Asher and the others were fucked up, of course they were fucked up, but she didn't know how to get through to them through the shock. Fuck, this wasn't what she was good at.

"They're gone?"

"For now, I think. They seem to come out at night," she said and hoped that she wasn't wrong.

Asher nodded and got lost in looking around at the blood and carnage around the station. Fuck, they needed to get out of the damn station. Ivy kept her focus on Asher.

"How badly are you all hurt? Can you walk or do we need to figure that out?" Ivy asked.

"I ... I think we can go," Asher said.

"Good, just ... let's get you three cleaned up so we don't attract anything out there and maybe get some food ... "

"How can you think of food? What is wrong with you?" Asher asked.

"Look, we need to be practical about this. We've lost a lot of guards, and if we don't want to join the dead, we need to move forward," Ivy said.

Asher shook his head. "Fine, let's get out of here."

Ivy tried to ignore the looks Asher and the others were giving her as she raided the kitchen. She hadn't eaten in hours, and it was going to be a hike back to Mid Station, so she needed something to eat. It would do the others no good to pass out or be too weak to fight when the things came back again. It was the only thing she could do to keep sane. Do something normal, don't think about the blood and the guts and the people they once were. In the kitchen, doing something normal, she could almost pretend she was shaking because she was hungry.

"I don't think we should leave," Asher said.

"We have to. Marcus isn't believing what's going on, and we have to tell him he's full of shit, though maybe not exactly that way," Ivy said.

"They'll come for us," Asher said.

"Probably not in time. We need to be back at Mid by nightfall," Ivy said. Ivy knew that Asher was still in shock over the whole situation and that people reacted differently, but they really needed to be practical about the fucking thing if they didn't want to join the dead.

"I ... I don't ... "

"Asher. We need to leave this place, and if you don't want to fucking die, you should come with me. I'll give you a little time,

I want to look around at something outside the station, but you really need to come with me if you want to live."

Asher nodded and Ivy hoped that he would come. She could give him a little longer. It was still early in the morning, and it didn't take that long to get to Mid Station.

Ivy had seen the trail of blood leading to the cave in the early morning light, and she felt the need to investigate. She had little hope of finding anyone alive, but then again, the creatures had left her and not come back, and Zero and Calla had found her.

Ivy followed the trail of blood toward a cave entrance she knew was too small for a person to enter, and she wasn't going to fucking die squeezing herself into a cave.

"You little fuckers," Ivy said. There were flies and bugs of all sorts flying around the mouth of the cave. There was a lot of blood and bits of flesh and bone. She lifted a hand to cover her nose.

"Disgusting. Fascinating," Ivy said. Well, there wouldn't be anyone left alive after being dismembered and dragged into a cave. Ivy looked around. There was an entrance to the cave nearby that she could go into, and it would get her close to where the creatures had entered. She started out that way, unsure if she was going to actually go in. It was probably stupid to go in alone with no one knowing where she was, but they were lacking information.

Ivy stood before the cave with a lantern in her hand. "Fuck it." Ivy had been in most of the caves in the area at least once.

She liked to take shelter in them when the weather was shitty, and they were fun to explore. As long as they were unoccupied.

Ivy entered the cave and went toward where the creatures had taken bits of bodies into the cave. As she got closer, she could smell the blood and a faint odor of apples. She drew her sword and slowed down. The passage she was following was wide enough for two men to walk side-by-side and was two feet or so taller than she was; enough room to move around if she needed to.

"Oh fuck," Ivy closed her eyes and turned away. A mass of flesh, almost impossible to tell that it was ever human, filled the tunnel to the left. There was no sign of where the creatures were. Every instinct told Ivy to run and get the fuck out of there, but she pressed forward down the tunnel to the right, which she knew she could follow for quite a while.

Ivy heard something ahead of her and stopped to listen, but she couldn't hear anything else. Ivy concentrated on where her lantern light was ahead of her and was ready to turn and run at the first sign of danger.

She was concentrating so hard on the light ahead that her foot hit a patch of slick blood.

"Fuck!" Ivy tried to right herself but fell to the ground, hard. The lantern slipped from her fingers and hit the stone floor. The base cracked and the oil leaked out, briefly illuminating the cavern in a burst of flame before burning out and plunging Ivy into total darkness.

Ivy didn't notice at first, too focused on the pain shooting up her leg from her ankle and the throbbing cut on her cheek. She blinked a few times.

"Oh fuck, fuck. Okay, stay calm. Calm. Think." Ivy tried to get her breathing under control as her heart pounded in her chest. She pulled herself into a sitting position and tried to think in total darkness. She could get out. It wouldn't be that hard to find her way back, as long as she picked the right direction to begin with.

"Think, Ivy," she muttered. She had been heading into the cave, down into the cave. She luckily had a waterskin with her. She put her hand on the cave floor and poured water over her hand; the water trickled down to her left.

"Left is down, the exit is to my right." She poured water twice more with her hand in slightly different parts of the cave floor and found the same result. She stood and turned to her right but nearly collapsed again when she put her full weight on her left ankle.

"Fuck me," she said. No use worrying about it at the moment, though; she couldn't see shit and didn't really want to feel if she had a bone sticking out or something. She kept her left hand on the cave wall for support as she slowly moved forward in the dark. She knew she would come to the passage on the left to get out, and she'd run into the pile of bodies before she got lost that way.

Ivy fought against the sense of panic. She couldn't see. She had gone into a cave and not told anyone. There were bloodthirsty creatures somewhere in the cave with her. She wouldn't be able to fight them if they came upon her.

"Stop fucking thinking about them," Ivy said.

What was she supposed to concentrate on? How much her ankle hurt? She went forward slowly and carefully, determined to get herself out of the stupid mess she had gotten herself into. And for nothing. Well, maybe not nothing. They did seem to like rotting meat and they went into the caves during the day. Hopefully that was worth it.

Ivy stepped wrong on her ankle and tried not to scream. She tried taking deep breaths through the lightning shots of pain going up to her hip and back down.

Ivy heard something behind her, an echo in the cave. She couldn't tell what it was or how close it was. She took another deep breath and moved forward. She needed to get out and she needed to get the information to the others even if it turned out to be useless.

She ... wanted to see the others. She wanted to see Calla in particular.

"Don't go there now," she thought. "Stupid."

It was true, though. Of all the people she knew, most would probably not really care if she didn't come back. She didn't exactly endear herself to people. But there was something about how Calla looked at her. She always smiled. She was kind even when Ivy was being a bitch.

"We have to do this now, brain," Ivy huffed as she pushed herself forward. It was distracting, at least; it was getting her to keep going. She heard another noise behind her. She pushed forward.

Finally she came to the turn. She could smell the rotting bodies in front of her as she turned into the tunnel she knew would lead her out. Ivy couldn't go very fast. She wanted to run but couldn't. She still thought she heard something behind her.

When she first saw light, she thought she might be imagining it. She held her hand out in front of her and she could see it; she was getting closer to the exit. She could smell fresh air.

Almost out.

There was something behind her. There was no mistaking it for imagination. There was a skittering sound. Too big to be bugs or rats. Too small to be a bear or big cat. Ivy tried to keep calm. If she could get a little further, there would be enough light for her to put up a little bit of a fight even if she was hindered by the ankle.

She pushed past the pain to get to the light.

Something was behind her. Close.

She wasn't going to look behind her until she had enough light to see. It wouldn't make any sense to turn around to face what she couldn't see.

Ivy could smell them now, the rotting apple scent wafting close behind her. At last she could see well enough to turn around and see if there really was anything behind her.

Three creatures. Ivy walked backward into the light as best she could, which was very awkward with the fucking ankle.

"Why are you little shits not attacking?" she asked them. Maybe they were full; they had a lot of nice rotting meat not far away and didn't really have to risk anything to kill her.

"Fuck off!" Ivy yelled at them, and they did nothing. Well, sound didn't seem to scare them off. Ivy continued backing up and hoped she didn't fall; she was sure that if she fell, that was going to be it.

Ivy risked a look behind her and realized she was almost out of the cave, almost into the full light. So of course Ivy had to fall. Her ankle gave out and she fell on her ass. She scooted back as much as she could into the light.

The creatures started to hiss and lunge forward a little bit, but they wouldn't get into the light. Ivy watched them for a few moments. Were they just playing, or did they really dislike the light so much as to avoid it? Or was it again because they weren't quite hungry? If they were starving, would they come out into the light?

Ivy pulled herself up with a groan, and the creatures still lunged, not quite into the light.

"I guess that means we're safe for the moment and you hate light," she said. At least sunlight. She wasn't sure if the light of torches would be enough, and there were always shadows to hide in.

"See you fuckers later," Ivy said and started to walk away. The creatures hissed and skittered in the shadows. They did not come after her even though she was limping and crying out in pain. That would attract any other hunter.

The light. She could use that if she could get back down to the others.

It was a struggle, but she made it back to the station and then got Asher and the others ready to go. She wrapped her ankle as best she could. At least it wasn't broken. Then they headed out. She knew even then that they wouldn't quite make it before dark. Hopefully they would have enough light around them or somehow beat the creatures back.

4

THE SECOND NIGHT

Calla sat down on the wooden bench across from Zero with a sigh. She didn't know what to say to Zero or what was going on. She didn't believe that Zero could be the cause of such carnage, and even though Ivy was a bit odd, she didn't think that Ivy would do something like that either.

Marcus had called her naive and told her she was easily swayed and that's why Zero took her with him. She didn't know what was and wasn't true.

"Calla?"

"I ... I don't know what is going on," she said.

"What did Marcus say?"

Calla took a deep breath. She didn't know how Zero could be so calm, sitting in a cell with Marcus out to harm him.

"He's convinced the slaughter was you and Ivy and that you chose me to witness it because I'm gullible and an easy mark," Calla said.

"Fuck him, you know I didn't do that, right?"

"I ... think I do. I'm so confused. You're up here for a reason and there are rumors."

Zero nodded. "Parts of the rumors are true. I was part of a training exercise where all my squad died. I nearly died."

"Why did they think you'd done it?"

Zero sighed. "Two days before the exercise, I put ink in everyone's canteens as a prank. On the mission, it was something in the water that poisoned us. I tampered with the water before, so they thought I'd done it again. Then there was the fact that I chose to live my life and not let myself be destroyed by the fact that I lived."

Calla nodded. "I can see how people could think that was suspicious."

"I don't know what happened that night. We all filled our own canteens. Whatever was in the water didn't take long. My mouth burned then went numb. Everything started to turn numb. We all vomited." Zero sighed. "None of us were well enough to start a fire, we were all freezing. I could barely move, I was lying still but my heart was racing. People started dying. I could hear their labored breathing suddenly stop, and I was sure I'd be dying soon. I didn't kill my friends."

"I'm sorry, Zero. I believe you. I'm sorry I couldn't convince Marcus."

"Don't worry about it," he said.

"I do. He's going to try to kill you," Calla said. "Ivy was sure I could do it, that's why she left."

"He can't kill me without a tribunal," Zero said.

"I know the rules, but … I think Marcus is willing to break them. And we still have the creatures to worry about."

Calla hoped that Ivy was having better luck than they were. She hoped that the creatures were nocturnal or at least had a small range or something else that would keep the other stations safe.

Calla tried to stay calm about the whole thing; Zero certainly was, but the day was passing by and she dreaded what night would bring.

It didn't look like anything was going to happen soon, though, and Calla tried to curl up in a comfortable position on the bench and get some rest. Maybe Marcus didn't believe there were monsters out there, but Calla knew better. Sleep would do her good.

Calla woke with a start, nearly falling off the bench as the door to the cell was opened.

"Have anything to say for yourself, Zero?" Marcus asked.

"No, sir, my statement remains the same," Zero said.

Marcus shook his head. "Have it your way." Marcus crossed the small cell in two steps and pulled Zero up off the bench by his collar. Calla was on her feet but couldn't do anything as Marcus punched Zero in the jaw, sending the man sprawling on the floor. Marcus took the opportunity to kick Zero in the stomach before backing up.

Zero groaned and coughed on the floor of the cell. Calla looked around. No one else was there.

"What do you say now, Zero?"

"Same thing, sir," Zero said quietly.

Marcus grabbed Zero off the floor and pulled his fist back again.

"Stop!" Calla cried out. "Sir, this is against the rules."

Marcus scoffed, dropping Zero on the bench. "You simple, idealistic, naive cunt. You think rules really work in the real world? This man is a murderer. He got out of punishment once before, and I will not let that happen again!"

"Sir ... "

"Do you want to join him? It would be easy for me to charge you with helping him."

"This is wrong," Calla said, voice shaking. She looked at Zero. She didn't know what to do. Marcus was twice her size and armed. She wasn't much of a fighter, truth be told. She wasn't much of anything.

"Calla, I'm going to make this very clear. I order you to leave this cell and wait in the mess hall."

"No, sir."

Calla was shaking, and she couldn't help the tears that ran down her cheeks. She wasn't going to leave Zero alone to be beaten to death.

Marcus looked between her and Zero. "You know, maybe you are right, Calla. This should be more of an example."

"Sir ... "

" ... and I'm well within my rights to have him flogged. And I don't need a tribunal for that."

"I ... " Calla couldn't stop it. She didn't know how to stop it without causing more trouble for herself and Zero. She looked down at Zero with his swollen jaw and didn't know what to do.

Marcus pulled Zero off the ground and pushed Calla aside. Everything was happening so fast that none of it made sense. She couldn't help but follow and watched as Marcus tied Zero to the pole. Calla didn't even know if anyone had ever been flogged in all her years there. Several people came out to see what was going on. No one seemed eager to stop it.

"Calla," Zero said.

"I don't ... I'm sorry ... I ... "

"It'll be night soon," Zero said.

"But ... "

"I can survive this, let's not ... "

"Shut up!" Marcus said, slapping Zero across the face. "And you'd better step back, Calla."

She did. She stepped back. She wanted to stop it, but Zero did have a point. If Marcus got any more riled up about the whole thing, he might lash out and kill Zero. This was horrible, but it was survivable.

The first hit of the lash made Calla jump almost as much as Zero. He grunted in pain, blood blooming across his back.

Another hit, more blood. Zero grunted again.

The third hit cut into one of the previous lashes, and Zero screamed in pain. He was shaking as blood ran down his back. Calla put a hand over her mouth; she was afraid she was going to be sick.

He screamed again as the fourth strike hit him, and it looked like he wanted to go to his knees, but with the way he was tied, he could not do so.

Marcus took his time between the fourth and fifth strike so when he finally brought the lash down, Zero screamed and writhed on the pole.

"There, all in accordance with the rules, and I can do this again in the morning," Marcus said. He rolled up the bloody whip then loosened the restraints, so Zero could fall to his knees. Then Marcus left without a word to anyone.

Zero was slumped against the pole, bloody and tired. They had maybe a half hour before dark. Calla approached Zero and knelt in front of him. He was still shaking and pale, and there were streams of blood running down his back, but his cuts weren't too deep, and it was unlikely they would prove difficult to heal.

Calla wiped tears from her face and took a deep breath.

"I'm going to get you some water," Calla said.

"Thank you," Zero said.

Calla felt shaky and sick as she entered the main room. Marcus was there, tucking into his dinner, and Calla couldn't believe he could just sit down and eat after torturing Zero all afternoon.

Calla wondered what had become of Ivy; had she run off or gotten killed? Everyone else looked a little stressed but probably because of the torture going on and not a sense of dread. Calla grabbed some supplies before heading back to Zero.

"I got you some water, a little soup if you can eat. I'll clean you up a bit," Calla said. "I'm sorry." She lifted the cup of water to his lips to help him drink. Then she cleaned some of the blood off Zero's back, as gently as she could.

"I have a feeling this will be over soon," Zero said. "At nightfall."

"You think the creatures will come?"

"Yes," Zero said.

"On the one hand, I hope not, but on the other, I don't want to see Marcus kill you. I ... don't know what else to do," Calla said.

"It's good to know that at least one person has my back," Zero said. A back that was currently torn open and bleeding.

"I think more would if they weren't so scared of Marcus," Calla said. She had brought bandages with her and a shirt and managed to get things wrapped up a little. Getting the shirt on over the manacles was harder, but at least Zero wouldn't be shivering in the night air. Calla sat with Zero, intending to keep her promise of not leaving his side. She was beginning to consider how far she was willing to go with it. She was near the point where she wanted to put herself between Marcus and Zero no matter the cost. Everyone else seemed scared and indifferent to the whole thing. Maybe if Calla was hurt, they would stand up to Marcus.

"Fuck," Zero said, looking around suddenly.

"Zero?"

"I smell them," he said.

"You're sure?"

"Yes." Zero pulled his hands and the chains rattled. "Marcus has the key?"

"Yes, I'll sound the alarm," Calla said. She couldn't smell the apple scent, but she believed that Zero could. The alarm bell was across the courtyard from where Zero was tied up. Calla rang it then started back to Zero.

"What is the meaning of this?" Marcus demanded.

"The creatures are coming," Calla said. "We're soon to be under attack."

Marcus stood stock-still and stared at Calla. She swallowed hard. She had to stand her ground; she knew that they were in danger, and everyone needed to know it.

"This is sedition. You and Zero are charged with sedition, and it is my right to take out a threat to the guard," Marcus said, drawing his sword. Calla's hand went to her own sword, but she stopped. If she drew against Marcus, there was no doubt about what she was doing.

"We are in danger from creatures that have killed an entire station before. We haven't had contact with West Station. One or two people could not have caused the slaughter I saw. I know it's hard to believe, but Zero and I are telling the truth. I'm not trying to betray the guard, I'm trying to save us!" Calla let out a frustrated sigh as tears started to slip down her cheeks. Of course she couldn't even stand up for things without crying. Stupid. She wiped the tears away.

Marcus took a swing at her with his sword, and Calla jumped back. She looked at all the gathered guards behind Marcus, hoping that at least one of them would intervene. She could see confusion and uncertainty on most people's faces, so that was something, at least. Calla continued to back up toward Zero.

She was only a few steps in front of Zero, and Marcus was still advancing with his sword drawn. Well, she wasn't going to give in. She couldn't let Marcus kill Zero.

"This is your last chance, Calla. Stand down now, and I'll only expel you from the guard. This is all Zero's doing. Stand aside, Calla."

"No."

"So be it," Marcus said. Up until the last second, Calla hoped that Marcus would stop or someone else would stop him. Marcus lunged forward, and Calla drew her sword and blocked him.

The station door burst open behind Marcus, and Ivy and three other guards came in.

"What the fuck ... "

"You! Someone get her before she escapes," Marcus ordered.

"Those things are right behind us," Ivy said.

"They killed all but three of us at West Station," Asher said. "What the hell is going on here? Why aren't you preparing for an attack?"

"You ... you're all in on this," Marcus said.

"You're in the wrong, Captain," Calla said. "You have more witnesses now. Let Zero go and let's get ready for ... "

Someone screamed in the crowd. Calla realized she could smell rotting apples. Ivy was wrong, they weren't coming. They were already there.

Calla saw another guard go down, swarmed by five of the creatures at once. They were real, she had been right. Zero was right. Ivy was right.

"Marcus ... "

More screams as another guard went down.

"Marcus, I need the key," Calla said. Marcus looked at her, at Zero, then turned around to face the onslaught of creatures.

"Shit!" Calla went to Zero and looked at the shackles. She knew good and well that there was no way she could get them off without a key, but she didn't know what else to do.

"Calla, get your sword!" Zero called out. She grabbed her sword and swung at the first creature to attack. Ivy was right, they looked quite feline. Longer claws, longer jaws, and an odd dark green, but very cat-like. Not solitary hunters like cats, though; they swarmed. That's how the others were slaughtered. Panicked and overwhelmed. And it was happening again.

Calla knocked another creature back as it jumped toward Zero. They were going to lose, going to be killed. There had to be something the creatures didn't like. Something fell near Calla, and she saw a torch from the wall knocked down and three of the creatures kicking dirt at it.

The light. They didn't like the light.

"Set things on fire, burn everything!" Calla yelled. She went for a torch and held it before her in her left hand and the sword in her right and tried to keep the creatures away from her and Zero.

She tried to spot where Marcus was in the fight; she still needed to get the shackle key off of him to free Zero.

A sudden burst of light erupted from the central tower. Good. Either someone heard her or figured it out themselves. The creatures screeched at the light and backed away from it. It didn't completely stop them, and Calla watched in horror as a guard was dragged into the shadows.

"Calla!"

"Ivy, did you set the blaze?"

"Yes. Where's the key?" Ivy nodded toward Zero.

"Marcus has them," Calla said.

"Fucker, I'll get it," Ivy said. The remaining guards, nine that Calla could see, were all heading for the light as the creatures backed away from it. Marcus was still alive, and several guards, including Ivy, were surrounding him and shouting.

Marcus came toward them, and for a second, Calla thought he might be coming in to try to kill them, but then he took the key out and released Zero. Zero fell slightly, and Calla dropped her torch to support him.

"We'll talk about this later," Marcus said. Calla nodded but kept her attention on Zero. There was a patch of darkness they needed to cross to get to the others and safety.

"We have to move fast, Zero, I'm sorry," she said.

"I can do it," he said, but he stumbled slightly as they started to move.

"We've got you!" Ivy called out, and Calla and Zero ran. Calla could hear the creatures leap forward — she thought she might have felt one try to grab at her ankle as she passed — but she made it into the light with Zero.

She turned to see if Marcus had made it, just in time to watch two of the creatures drag him down. Calla made sure Zero wasn't going to fall over and ran toward Marcus as he was being dragged away.

Calla cut down one of the creatures and managed to grab Marcus and started to drag him back into the light. Asher and Ivy came forward to help her, and they managed to get him back.

"Oh fuck," Ivy said, and Calla looked down.

Blood was pouring from Marcus' neck where the creatures had torn into him. Zero quickly clamped both hands on the bleeding wound, his hands instantly soaked in blood.

"He's losing too much blood," Zero said.

"Do we have a healer here?" Calla asked as she looked away.

The answer was no. Calla didn't think a healer could do anything as quickly as Marcus was losing blood.

"Med kit?" Zero asked.

"Across the way," someone said, pointing past a very dark patch with several creatures milling about in it.

Calla swallowed. "I'll get it." Marcus grabbed her with a shaking hand and shook his head no and frantically looked between Zero and Calla.

"Fuck," Zero said. "Don't go for it, Calla."

Calla nodded. Marcus was fading quickly, eyes dim and wandering as he took shallow gasps of air. Calla took his hand and held it in hers. It was only another minute or so until Marcus went still.

Zero stood, looking at the huddled guards. With Marcus and the station's lieutenant gone, Zero was the highest-ranking guard. Back wrapped in bloody bandages, covered in the captain's blood, Zero looked at them all and spoke.

"We keep the fire burning and stick to the light. The creatures have to go somewhere before dawn, then we'll figure out what comes next."

It seemed like such a simple order, but Calla thought this would likely be the longest night of her life.

The creatures tried again and again to pull people into the darkness, to kick dirt on the fire to put it out, to jump and catch them by surprise. They succeeded a few times.

Calla caught sight of one of the things about to jump on Zero and managed to pull him back and slice the creature enough to get it to run away.

"Thanks," he said.

"Hanging in there?"

"Trying," he said. More creatures, more fighting. The night seemed endless.

About an hour before dawn, the creatures started to leave, taking bits of bodies with them as they went. That was particularly hard to watch.

Dawn came at last. Calla was alive. Zero was alive, Ivy and Asher were still alive. There were eight of them left alive.

Just two days before, there were thirty-six guards spread out along the Caldera stations. Now there were eight, and most of them were wounded.

"Right. We need to take care of the wounded, then pack up and head to the fort and regroup," Zero said.

"We're just going to leave the dead?" Asher asked. "Again. I'm not surprised Ivy was like that, but I thought better of you."

"I would love to be able to bury the dead, but we need to leave," Zero said. "We need to get help for those of us who are still alive."

"I still don't like it."

"Neither do I," Zero said, "but it is what we have to do."

Calla took stock of her own wounds. Scratches and bruises, not much else. She was extremely lucky.

"Are you alright?" Ivy asked.

"Yeah, most of this isn't my blood. I noticed you limping."

"Twisted my fucking ankle trying to track the creatures into the cave," Ivy said. "They go into the caves during the day and don't like coming out in the light. We should be safe now."

"We know a little more, I guess. I … don't know what we're going to do," Calla said.

"I don't know either. Zero's back looks bad."

"He claims it's not as bad as it looks," Calla said.

"We're going to have to stand up for him again."

"Probably," Calla said. She didn't want to have any other arguments about what was going on. She was really sick and tired of it. They needed to do something, not argue about what was happening.

It didn't take long for them to get ready to leave; even those who were hurt the worst wanted to get away from the station and get back to the fort. Calla wanted to get back to her room at the fort, and she wanted to take a nap. She wanted to sleep for several days, but that wasn't going to be possible. They had to act fast if they were going to stop the creatures from spreading further west.

Calla walked near the back of the group with Ivy, who was still limping even though they had wrapped her ankle. No one really felt like talking. It was quite the somber procession coming down from the station.

They were halfway down to the fort when Zero stopped. Calla made her way up to the front.

"I smell blood," he said, "fresh."

"I don't, but I trust that you do," Calla said. She drew her sword. There shouldn't be any creatures out and about, but just in case.

"Move on, eyes open," Zero called behind him.

They only had gone a little bit more when they heard someone calling out for help. Calla thought she recognized the voice. It was a human voice, that was certain. They pushed forward toward the voice.

"Help!"

Ramona. It was Ramona, but what was she doing out in the forest away from the fort?

"Ramona!" she called out.

"Calla? Help!"

Calla followed the sound of her voice and came to a thick patch of trees not far off the main path. The grass was slick with blood, and there were parts of bodies all around.

"Ramona!" Calla cried as she caught sight of the healer sitting up against a tree.

"Calla. I ... I ... We saw the fire, we tried to come see what was going on," Ramona said.

"How many from the fort came with you?" Zero asked.

"All but five," Ramona said. "What ... what ... "

"Calla? Can you look around for anyone else alive?"

"I will," Calla said. She didn't think she would find anyone else, but she set about it methodically to make sure she didn't miss anywhere. She tried to keep it out of her mind that Ramona said that there were only five people left at the fort. So they were down to fourteen people. And if the creatures got through them, they would spread out below the Caldera from village to village as far as the caves would allow them to, which was quite the distance. Once they spread, there would be no way to stop them. They needed to do something, but she didn't know what fourteen people, many of them wounded, could actually do.

Calla couldn't find any bodies, living or dead. She saw blood. Bits of bone.

"Calla!"

"Here!"

"Come back out, we need to move," Zero said.

"I didn't find anyone," Calla said. "Plenty of signs of where people fell but no one alive."

Zero nodded. "We'll figure it out once we get back to the fort. Let's get there and get people patched up and fed and see what we can do."

"Yes, sir," Calla said. Zero smiled at that. Calla usually didn't bother with honorifics. Most people at the Caldera didn't really worry about rank beyond the captain, but it felt like they needed a little more protocol with all that was going on.

The wounded, tired group made it back to the fort. It was clear once they got there that Zero was the highest-ranking officer left out of the group. Fourteen out of a hundred were alive.

Zero took charge the instant he got back. Calla had never seen him like that before. Calla helped Ramona with the wounded until they were taken care of, then went to the galley for some food, where Ivy was sitting alone.

"How's the ankle?"

"Still fucked, but a little better," Ivy said.

"Good."

"I'm glad you're alright, Calla," Ivy said. "I was worried when we saw the station under attack."

Calla smiled. "I was worried about you too."

"I shouldn't have gone into those caves alone. I broke my lantern about a mile in and had to backtrack through the dark and thought the creatures were gonna jump me at any second. I ... I was thinking about you, that I wanted to see you again."

Calla smiled. She hadn't thought that Ivy really liked her. It was a little overwhelming. "That's really sweet, Ivy."

"Don't tell anyone I fucking said that," Ivy said.

"Wouldn't dare," Calla replied.

5

— · —

NEW LEADERSHIP

Calla didn't think she would be able to get to sleep with all that had happened, but her exhausted body had other plans, and she more or less passed out. She knew she couldn't sleep long; a few hours, maybe. But there was going to be a lot to do before nightfall and a probable attack.

Calla wandered into the galley a little after noon to find Zero sitting with a cup of tea and staring at nothing. The fort was quiet; most were still sleeping or dealing with what had just happened.

"Morning, or afternoon, I suppose, sir," she said as she sat down. Zero looked ... well, he didn't look good, but he didn't look as bad as one might expect. Still, it looked like he could sleep for days.

"Thank you," Zero said.

"For?"

"Calling me sir. You've done it a few times now."

"Of course, you're our leader now," Calla said.

"For now." He sighed. "We have to get the word out, but I think it's too late in the day to send a messenger out; they won't make it down the hill before nightfall. So we'll have to survive tonight."

"We can set up enough fires, I think, we've got plenty of wood since we're stocked up for winter. I ... don't know what we'll do if we have to stay here all winter, but survival is our goal right now," Calla said.

"Agreed. We'll have to get going on it soon if fourteen wounded guards expect to get it done," Zero said.

"How are you feeling?"

"Better. Or at least not worse. Not looking forward to holding a meeting, but I need to," Zero said.

"I have your back and so does Ivy," Calla said. "We don't have time to fight each other."

"I know. We just have to convince everyone else," Zero said.

"The chain of command is a thing for a reason, and you're doing an excellent job so far," Calla said.

"Thanks, Calla."

An hour later, they were all gathered in a room that could hold a hundred people but now held less than a quarter of that. Zero stood up at the podium and looked at the gathered guards.

"First order of business is to get this fort ready for nightfall," Zero said.

"Shouldn't we go get help?" Ramona asked.

"I doubt anyone could make it down by nightfall, and I don't want to risk a messenger getting killed *en route*."

"Wait ... wait, isn't there something else we need to discuss? Is he really the one to lead us?" Asher asked.

"Captain Marcus is dead, so are the other lieutenants. The chain of command falls to me," Zero said. "We don't have time to bicker if we want to live. If, after this is all over, you wish to lodge a complaint, please do so, but for now, we need to focus on staying alive."

"I don't think a man who killed his entire platoon as a joke should lead," someone else said.

"My leadership is not up for discussion," Zero said.

"How do we know you didn't kill Marcus?"

"Because a creature ripped the captain's throat out, you fucking idiot," Ivy said. "I saw it happen and so did Calla."

"I still think someone should be able to get to town before dark," Ramona said.

"I won't risk it," Zero said, "and we need everyone here to prepare for tonight. There aren't many of us left, and I don't want to lose anyone else if I can help it."

"We should all just leave," Asher said.

"We can't make it down by nightfall, not with so many of us hurt," Ivy said.

"We can't do this," Asher said.

"We must," Zero said.

"We can't lead those things down the hill," Calla said.

"Do you really think we can stop them?"

"We have to try," Zero said. "That is our duty as guards."

"Our duty to die?" Asher scoffed.

"It is our duty as guards to protect people. Calla is right. We can't lead those things to other people without trying to dispose of them first. We will send for help, but we need to hold this fort at the very least. We all swore an oath when we joined that we would lay down our lives to protect others. I will do everything in my power to prevent that from happening, but I will uphold my oath of protection to whatever end."

"As will I," Calla said.

"Well, fuck, how could I not after a speech like that," Ivy said. There were murmurs of agreement in the crowd and then silence as Zero waited to see if anyone else would speak up.

"We need to get to work protecting the fort. We're going to line the entire wall with fire so those bastards won't want to try to attack us."

"We should have lantern oil ready to relight as well. I saw some of the creatures trying to put out fires last night, they're not stupid," Calla said.

"Good point," Zero said. "We'll do that. Let's get started, then. Calla, hang back a moment, I have something to ask you."

Calla nodded and couldn't help but feel a little nervous. She knew it was stupid, but that was just the way she was sometimes.

"Thank you for your support again," Zero said.

"Of course," she said.

"I hope we can fend those things off tonight, but if I die, I need someone to lead, and I would like you to do it."

"Me?" She scoffed and shook her head.

"Yes, Calla, you have a good head on your shoulders. No one would argue with you leading, and I know Ivy would have your back. I need to make sure that someone is going to be able to lead if I die."

"I don't know if I'm qualified to do it," Calla said.

"You are. I would really like it to be you. I trust you to get the others to safety and keep a cool head," Zero said.

"Alright. I accept. But I really don't want to do it, so you'd better not die, Zero," she said.

Zero snorted. "I'll be sure to try."

Calla really hoped that she wouldn't have to take over. Even with a small group, she didn't think she could do it. It felt good to have Zero express confidence in her, but she didn't quite believe it herself.

She tried to ignore that particular anxiety and concentrate on getting the fort ready. They had a winter's worth of wood at the fort, which looked like it was going to be enough to have the fire burning all night.

They had a decent amount of lantern oil that could be used to quickly set things ablaze if they needed to. It all looked like it would work, but Calla thought they should still be very cautious about it since they didn't really know all that much about the creatures.

Or maybe she had just read too many stories and the creatures were simple in essence, but it was the amount of them that was the problem.

There were plenty of unknowns, though; how fast did they move, how much did they have to eat, how fast did they reproduce. It wasn't as if she'd had the chance to look closer and pick out any young while they were ripping her friends apart.

By supper time, they had the fort set for the night.

"Well, I think that's the best we can do," Zero said.

"I think it looks good," Calla said.

"I hope so. We just have to make it through the night with at least one person to get down and warn everyone else in the morning. Of course, I don't want to lose anyone," Zero said.

"I know that, Zero," Calla said.

"I'm going to assign Asher to the tower," Zero said. "So he can lock himself in there if worse comes to worse, and then he can go down to the village to warn people. I ... I can't be the only survivor again. I wish I could put you all in the tower, but I don't think Asher is up to the fight that might hit us, and you and Ivy are."

"I wouldn't want to be in the tower, anyway," Calla said. "And you're right about Asher. I would say put Ivy up there, but with her ankle being messed up, she might not get to the village in time to warn them."

"That's what I was thinking. Plus I really think she wants to kill those things, as many of them as she can," Zero said.

"Yes. I want to as well," Calla said.

"Me too," Zero said. "As many as it takes to protect people."
They fell into silence for a little bit until Ivy came up and sat
down with her tray.

"So, assuming we don't get ripped apart for food tonight, I
have an idea," Ivy said.

"Alright, go on," Zero said.

"Since they spend the day in the cave, that's probably how
they came out. That earthquake must have opened a passage in
the caves from wherever they are. We need to find that place,
where they sleep."

"Go into the caves," Zero said.

"I know it sounds insane," Ivy said.

"It is insane," Zero said.

"I know, but if we can block where they are coming from ...
"

"If they go back to the same place," Calla said.

"That's what we need to know," Ivy said.

"I'm assuming you want to use fire powder to block them
in."

"Of course," Ivy said.

"Do we have any experts in fire powder, or are we winging it?"
Calla asked.

"I know enough," Zero said with a smile.

"That is disturbing," Ivy said.

"Disturbing but useful," Zero said.

"It might work," Calla said. "And destroying them before they have time to settle in, as it were, would be the best course of action. I hate the idea of just sitting around, waiting for another night of hell."

"Alright, we'll think on the idea. First things first, we have to survive tonight. I'm going to have everyone up on the wall and Asher in the tower. We have to keep the fires burning, and we need to have eyes on where the creatures are. I don't want to be caught by surprise. I want to know what those fuckers are doing. Calla and I will be walking the walls and checking in to see if we have any problem areas where we need more people. How's your ankle, Ivy?"

"Fucked but not bad, I'll be able to stand and fight," she said.

"Good."

"I'll push through this," Ivy said. "Tonight and when we go into the caves."

Zero nodded. "Good."

Calla wished there was more time to plan and time to rest; they only had a little bit of time to take a nap before they needed to be up and ready. Well, she supposed it was better than nothing.

Zero took the east and south walls, and Calla was on the west and north walls. Four people per wall seemed like it would be enough. It seemed a bit silly, actually; in all the training exercises, they had had two people per wall if there was nothing going on, and there was normally one person on the whole wall at night on a regular night.

They lit the fires just as the sun was sinking below the horizon. It was going to be hard to see the creatures until they were right on the fort, and Calla wondered if even Zero would have trouble smelling them with all the smoke in the air.

Now it was just a waiting game to see if the creatures would come. Calla had no doubt they would but really, really hoped that they wouldn't. One would think nearly a hundred people would be enough food for them, and they wouldn't need to hunt again.

Unless ... oh fuck, what if it was more a territorial thing? Had they thought of that before? Everything was starting to blur and go mad in her mind.

"Calla?"

"Sorry, what was that?"

"Nothing, you just stopped dead in your tracks and stared off into the distance," Ivy said.

"I did. I was just wondering if those things are being territorial and that's why they keep coming after us."

"Hmm, you would think they've had enough to eat," Ivy said.

"Exactly."

"Fuck, all the more reason to kill them off as quickly as possible," Ivy said.

"I wonder what kills them or keeps them in check in the Caldera?" Calla asked.

"I really don't want to think about that right now, Calla," Ivy said.

"Sorry, couldn't help it," she said. "I ... "

"Wait a second, I think we've got something out there," Ivy said. Calla peered with Ivy out past the light and the smoke and saw at least three pairs of eyes glowing in the dark tree line. Calla's heart started to pound.

"That's them," Calla said. "I'll go tell Zero and pass it on." Calla spread the word as quickly as she could and let Zero know.

"Surprised Asher didn't see them in the tower," he said.

"I think Ivy's part cat and can see in the dark," Calla said, and Zero snorted a laugh. Within the hour, the creatures were all around the fort in the forest. Calla walked the walls and waited. It didn't look like they were up to anything, but it wasn't like the guards knew how they hunted and acted. She found herself looking closer to the fire and even up in the air. She wondered if they could tunnel, or if they were smart enough to do things like that. She wondered how they communicated, and if there would be some sort of tell before they attacked.

There really wasn't; a group of ten of the creatures came out from the woods screeching and tried to kick dirt on the burning logs.

Calla was walking near Ivy when a few more tried it.

"Watch this," Ivy said and took a cup of lantern oil and tossed it at the creatures. The oil hit them and they burst into flames.

"Shit ... "

"Ha ha ha, you fuckers! Burn!" Ivy cackled. The creatures howled and dropped a few feet away from the burning logs. More creatures came out and tried to kick their fallen comrades into the fire as if that might put it out, which only made them burn more.

"They kind of smell like roasting apples," Calla said.

"They do." Ivy laughed.

Calla felt hopeful about the fires and their ability to keep the creatures out. But as the night wore on, the creatures got more riled up. They hissed and growled and made a strange howling noise.

"Ah fuck!"

Calla turned to see Ivy stepping back and using her sword to cut one of the creatures in half.

"They're jumping through the fire!" Ivy called out.

Three more creatures launched over the wall, and Calla looked over the edge to see how the hell they were doing it. They were standing on each other, and the creature on top was jumping over the flames and scaling the wall.

It was frightening and weird but fairly easy to see coming.

Calla met Zero to check in as the occasional creature came over the wall.

"I feel like we're not seeing something," he said.

"I know, but I can't figure out what it is," Calla said.

"I guess just keep your eye out," Zero said. More creatures came over, more creatures tried to put the fires out. Ivy and several others were pouring lantern oil to burn some of the creatures and keep the fires lit.

Calla saw a creature coming toward her and split it in half with her sword. Something hit her and she fell back and rolled off the wall and hit the ground below.

Calla's vision blurred and she couldn't breathe. The creature that hit her growled nearby; she couldn't really see where it was exactly and was having trouble moving at all. She patted the ground for her sword and couldn't find it. She drew her knife but knew she wouldn't have much reach with the damn thing. Her hand was shaking and her lungs just wouldn't draw in any air. She didn't know how badly hurt she was, if she had just knocked the wind out of herself or if she'd broken something. Perhaps many things.

The creature jumped up on Calla's chest, and she took a swing at it but didn't have the strength to land the strike.

Calla couldn't call out for help, but surely someone had seen her fall? The creature flexed its claws, and Calla felt her flesh tearing. The creature reared up to go for her throat, and Calla struck with her knife with as much force as she could.

The creature screeched as the knife pierced its belly. It stumbled away and died. Calla still couldn't quite move, but it didn't seem like there were any more creatures around.

"Calla!" Ivy was there with a lantern, looking at the blood on Calla while Calla tried to speak and tell her that most of the blood was the creature's and not hers.

"I ... "

"It's alright, I'll get Ramona," Ivy said.

"I'm okay," Calla managed.

"Are you?" Ivy asked. Calla nodded. Ivy didn't seem sure and examined the wounds the creature made and searched to make sure the blood wasn't Calla's blood.

"I'm okay," Calla repeated.

"Fuck. I think you are. Fuck, I thought that thing had got you," Ivy said.

"Help me up," Calla said.

"If you're sure."

Calla nodded. She still felt a little shaky but could breathe again. Ivy helped her back onto the wall, and the night continued.

6

— · —

TRACKING

Ivy watched Calla go down and thought it was all over. She had to run quite a ways to get to the stairs and by the time she had, the creature was dead, but Calla was still very still and covered in blood. Ivy shook as she knelt next to Calla to survey the damage.

By some miracle, Calla was alive and only slightly injured. Ivy tried to keep an eye on her the rest of the night.

By dawn, they were all still alive. The creatures started to creep back into the shadows of the forest as the light started to penetrate it. When she was sure the creatures were headed back and the light was growing brighter, she went to Zero.

"I need to leave soon if I'm going to track them. I … probably need help, just in case," she said.

"I'll come," Calla said.

"You're hurt," Ivy said.

"You are too, Ivy," Calla said.

"True. If you think you're up to it," Ivy said, "and Zero approves."

"I do, I can hold the fort," he said. "You two be careful. I need you both to come back."

"Yes, sir," Calla said.

"Might want to get the powder ready so we can get them before tonight, if we're lucky," Ivy said.

Zero nodded, then rubbed at the dark circles under his eyes. "Good luck."

Ivy gathered her things as quickly as she could and met Calla at the door of the fort, where Asher was also waiting to go out to warn the nearest village of what was going on.

"You two are fucking insane," Asher said.

"Probably," Ivy said. She didn't have time to deal with Asher, not again. The man didn't like her very much, anyway, and she was rather neutral towards him. She just hoped he would be able to get back to the village and warn people in time. Hopefully he wouldn't come upon an entire village of corpses. Ivy shivered at the thought.

"You alright?" Calla asked.

"Yeah, just had an unpleasant thought," she said.

Calla chuckled. "Imagine that."

"Fuck off," Ivy said and smiled when Calla smiled.

Ivy knew where the creatures were most likely headed and which route they would take: through the darkest parts of the forest to avoid the light. Ivy decided to take a path close to that but with a little more light. The last thing they needed was to walk right into an ambush. The creatures weren't stupid. They were fucking nuts but not stupid.

"I wish we could have brought Zero for his nose," Calla said. "I keep thinking I'm smelling them, but I'm not sure if it's real or not."

"Probably is," Ivy said. "We just need to be as careful as we can."

Calla grunted in response, and Ivy looked over at her to make sure that she was alright. She looked like she was holding up pretty well. Ivy was about the same. They were both exhausted, running on just enough food and rest to keep them alive. Ivy might have been able to stay up for a few days when she was in her twenties, but her forty-something body was protesting it hard.

"You know what? I don't think I'm ever going to be able to eat apples again after this," Ivy said.

Calla laughed. "Probably not."

"Fucking sucks too. I love apple pie."

"Now I'm hungry," Calla said.

"Maybe we'll catch one of those things and roast it on a spit," Ivy said. "Alive." Calla laughed again.

Ivy walked on with Calla by her side. Normally when someone was with her, she felt uncomfortable and annoyed. Not when it was Calla. Fuck, Ivy hoped that they would actually live through the whole thing, and maybe she and Calla could be more than just fellow guards.

Ivy caught a whiff of apples stronger than before and stopped to look around. The path ahead led through a dark copse of trees, but it was the best way to get where they were going.

"Swords out, I think," Ivy said. She wished there was another way to go, but if they were going to get to the cave in time to track the fuckers, they needed to go straight up. Ivy and Calla walked side by side with swords drawn, looking in every direction to try to spot movement. The coloration of the fucking things made sense; the dark green was perfect camouflage in the shadows of the forest.

A slight rustle was the only warning they got before two creatures lunged out of the bushes and another dropped down from one of the trees. Ivy managed to kill two and Calla the other before they moved forward slowly. They just needed to get to the top of the hill, and they would be in the open sunshine and be able to see the entrance to the cave Ivy was sure the creatures would be going into.

Another creature burst out of the bushes and missed Ivy's arm by inches.

At last, they were at the top of the hill in the sunshine; if there were any more creatures in the forest, they wouldn't dare come out in the bright morning light. Ivy walked to the edge of the depression. The rocky entrance to the cave was a good twenty feet below them and still bathed in shadow.

"Oh fuck," Ivy whispered as she looked at the creatures milling about the cave below. She felt frozen looking down at them. Calla touched her, and she nearly jumped out of her skin.

"At least two hundred," Calla whispered.

If the creatures caught sight of them, if they could stand the light, they would be dead and picked clean in a matter of minutes. And they were going to go into the caves with a few lanterns and torches to track the fucking things. It was madness.

"Are we really going to go in there?" Calla whispered.

"Fuck, I don't know. I might have another entrance point in mind," Ivy said. "I really don't want to go in there."

"If you have another idea, I'd like to try it," Calla said.

Ivy nodded. Waiting until all those things went in and then following them was starting to look like a really stupid idea. There was another entrance to the cave system and one closer to the area where the creatures probably came from. They attacked East Station first, so it made sense for them to have come from that area. Ivy hoped that she was right about it. She was used to tracking things and finding her way, and the wilderness had always made more sense than people.

Ivy hoped that the creatures made just enough sense that they could figure out how to kill them, where to kill them. The sun rose higher in the sky and the light came shining through the forest, and it felt much safer. Not safe enough to completely ignore the possibility of attack but enough that they could move faster.

They made it to the opening, a narrow split in the rocks that one could easily miss. Ivy had been in that particular cave several times. She often was out and about in the forest when storms would hit and knew good places to shelter.

"That's it?" Calla shifted and looked around.

"Yep, I know it doesn't look like much, but it'll do," Ivy said.

"If you say so," Calla said. They lit their lanterns, two torches, and grabbed some extra wood in case they were under for too long.

"Well, here we go," Ivy said.

"Please tell me we don't have to squeeze through narrow passages or swim under anywhere."

"Some areas are small, but I would say no squeezing. Shouldn't be much water this time of the year. I wouldn't want to try this one in spring."

The entrance narrowed a bit and sloped down into the cave system. Luckily there was only one way to go. There were other places in the system where one could easily get lost. Some people didn't have a good sense of direction underground, or at all, really, but Ivy was still as good underground as she was above it, maybe even better.

The air grew still and stale as they descended. Sound was strange underground. If their lights went out, it would go completely dark. Ivy had a little anxiety over the thought of it.

She didn't want a repeat of the last time she was following the fucking things.

"The main passage is just around another bend. There's a little drop, so we'll approach slowly so we know if it's safe to drop down."

"Can the creatures get up if they can see us?"

"Maybe, it's a bit of a drop, but they'll try."

They heard the creatures, and smelled them, before they saw them. They were hissing and chittering as they moved through the tunnel. For the longest time, Ivy and Calla stayed just around the corner where the creatures hopefully wouldn't come after them. Hopefully the light was enough to deter them.

They waited a long time until the hissing stopped. Ivy took a deep breath, hand on her sword as they rounded the corner. Ivy couldn't see anything at the opening to the drop, and she couldn't see anything down in the main passage. She took several deep breaths and only vaguely smelled apple.

"That's quite a drop," Calla said.

"For a short person, maybe," Ivy said. "I'll help you down and back up."

Ivy dropped a torch down and waited just a little longer to make sure there were no creatures before she dropped down and helped Calla down.

"Alright, forward we go."

"How much longer is this passage?"

"There's a big opening maybe a mile ahead. That's where I think they are," Ivy said. "And I think we can trap them there because there is only one entrance."

"Hopefully," Calla said. They walked slowly, partly because they wanted to be cautious and partly because they were both hurting. But there was no one else who could be doing the job. Most of the people at the fort and stations never made it into more than one cave and probably went in to get out of the rain and only went in a little bit.

"Ivy?"

"Hmm?"

"You said this dead-ends, right? Like a big open room where all the things can fit?"

"Right."

"Then why is there light ahead?"

Ivy blinked and looked ahead. She blinked again. There looked to be sunlight, just a little bit, ahead of them. It wasn't light from the torches or lanterns.

"What the fuck," Ivy said.

"Maybe we found where they came through," Calla said. "Maybe the earthquake opened something, and now they can get through."

"Maybe."

They pressed on, and it was getting more and more obvious that it was sunlight coming into the cave. There were a few more twists until they got to the opening. Ivy paused and drew her sword, very uncertain as to what she was going to find.

There was so much light shining that there had to be an opening.

"Shit," Calla said. Ivy stared and waited for her mind to figure out what she was looking at. There was light shining in through a thick forest of trees, several of which didn't look like any trees that she knew. The trees around the Caldera were mostly pine, but these were deciduous and their leaves were just starting to turn. Any of the deciduous trees outside the Caldera were much further along.

"We're ... looking out into the Caldera," Ivy said.

In the distance, Ivy could see the other side of the Caldera rising above the trees, she could see the high walls all around it, but it was much, much bigger than she thought it would be. At the base of the nearest tree, there was an entrance to a burrow of some sort, perhaps a rabbit den. Birds were singing in the distance, familiar and yet a little off.

"That's amazing," Calla said. Ivy moved forward into the room, holding her torch high to try to figure out where the fucking creatures were hiding. The room was filled with light, so it was hard to believe that they were anywhere near.

"Where are you," Ivy muttered.

"Over here," Calla called out.

Right at the edge of the forest, there was a huge gash in the rock leading further downward. It was only maybe three feet wide but too long to fill in with anything. And it would still probably be easier to blow the tunnel just before it opened, but at least there were a few options.

"We should head back," Ivy said.

"Yes," Calla said.

Ivy looked beyond the cave into the Caldera and didn't want to go back. Every bone in her body told her to keep going forward, that this was a fantastic opportunity to explore somewhere no one had ever been.

"You know the old stories, Calla. Has anyone been out there?"

"No. And for good reason, probably. I bet the creatures crawl out of caves every night and attack whatever lives out there," Calla said.

"I want to go out there so bad," Ivy said.

"I know, I sort of do too. But we can't. If we just blow this entrance to their underground home, they can come out somewhere else and use the tunnel," Calla said. "We have to block it all."

Ivy sighed. She knew it was the right thing to do; they had to stop the creatures from coming out of the Caldera and killing people. Maybe someday they would be able to find a way in that didn't let the creatures out. Then they would be able to explore.

"Come on, Ivy, we really should be getting back," Calla said softly.

Ivy nodded, and they left the bright new world and went back into the cave system. Her ankle was starting to throb again, but she pushed on; they had to get back to the fort as quickly as possible, and then they would have to set off again to make sure they could blow the cave by nightfall.

It had to end. There was no other way. Ivy could devote time to finding a way into the Caldera once everyone else was safe. There had to be some way to get back in, but first they needed to take care of business.

Ivy and Calla pushed on through the darkness. When they came to the offshoot again, they decided to head out the main entrance, as the creatures were all gone and underground again.

Coming back out of the cave seemed to take less time than going in, even with both of them moving slower because of their wounds. Ivy wondered if they were going to get some sort of award for the whole thing or if they would just be ignored. Zero would likely get a captaincy after it was all said and done. Maybe. Unless people started turning on him again. One thing was for certain, if anyone told Ivy she would have to move away from the Caldera, she was going to quit the guard.

"Still thinking about the Caldera?"

"Yep. Probably will for a long time. I'm going to find another way in there and figure out how to do it without the creatures being able to get out. I'll work on it the rest of my life if I have to," Ivy said.

"I'd like to help. I'm curious about it too."

83

"Would you leave the guard to do it?"

"I don't know."

"We'll have to replenish the guards we lost. We lost almost everybody," Calla said.

"True. I don't know, if they offer me a promotion, I think I'll have to turn it down," Ivy said.

"Even if you serve under Zero?"

"Ehh, maybe, fuck, I don't know. I guess we need to concentrate on surviving the current mission."

"We'll have to get back here pretty fast, and none of us are in good shape," Calla said.

"And we have to hope the powder goes off right and we don't just bury ourselves under the Caldera."

"We might be walking in our own tomb," Calla said.

Ivy laughed. "You have a morbid streak a mile wide, Calla. It's cute." Calla scoffed.

Finally they came out into the light, and Ivy felt a little better. It was a nice bright day, and there was no way the creatures were out. It was just a nice walk back to the fort.

***

Zero was pacing around the top of the fort as they approached and visibly relaxed when he saw them, meeting them at the door.

"Please tell me you found something."

"We found a lot," Ivy said.

"The earthquake broke a wall in the cave, exposing the Caldera. There's a whole forest in there, a whole habitat. But we're going to have to blow the entrance to that chamber to be sure to block the creatures," Calla said.

"Shame, but we really need to finish this as soon as possible," Zero said.

"Did something happen while we were gone?" Ivy asked.

"Yes. A whole argument about whether or not we should wait for back up to attempt anything. Asher and a few others still aren't happy that I'm in charge," Zero said.

"We need to do this. I don't know if the wood can last another night," Calla said.

"And I think we survived that by dumb fucking luck to begin with. My vote goes to leaving as quickly as we can and blowing the fucking thing. They can get mad at us later. We don't want new people sitting around talking and debating and wasting time," Ivy said.

"I agree, but it might be just us three going," Zero said.

"I think we can do it," Ivy said.

"Yes," Calla said, "the fewer people go, the faster we'll be."

"I don't know what's going to happen once more guardsmen get here," Zero said.

"I don't fucking care," Ivy said.

"I do care a little," Calla said. "But this is the right thing to do. We need to get this done. Last night we had good luck. Tonight we might not."

"Alright, you two go get something to eat and a quick nap. I'll take care of gathering all the supplies," Zero said.

"Yes, sir," Ivy and Calla said at the same time.

Ivy was starving and could use a few days' worth of naps but a little one would do. Ivy and Calla ate as quickly as they could to maximize nap time.

"Do you want me to come wake you up if I get up first?" Calla asked.

"Might be easier if we, uh, slept in the same bed? Just sleeping, I'm too tired," Ivy said.

"That would be nice." Calla smiled and Ivy smiled back. Nice indeed, a little comfort before going to certain death.

7

BLOWING THE CAVE

Calla woke with Ivy's arms wrapped around her. She snuggled closer for a few moments. She knew that they both needed to get up and get ready for the upcoming mission. Calla hoped that all would go well and that there would be more time for her and Ivy. Calla smiled as Ivy slept beside her.

Calla had never really thought of being in a relationship before. She knew it was more important for a lot of people, but she'd always just thought if it happened, fine, and if not, fine. She suspected Ivy wasn't keen on relationships because she was not going to change herself to appeal to anyone and figured that no one would like her as she was.

Calla did. She very much liked Ivy just as she was.

"We should wake up," Calla said softly.

"No."

"I don't want to either, but we can't let Zero go by himself," Calla said.

"We can," Ivy said then sighed. "No, I guess we can't. He'd probably get lost in the caves."

"Probably," Calla said. She got up first and got dressed, trying to ignore her bandaged wounds and how it still ached to breathe too deeply. She watched Ivy get out of bed, stepping gingerly on her ankle and rubbing her arm.

Zero didn't look much better; there were dark circles under his eyes, his left eye was still swollen, and his lip was split.

Ivy snorted. "We're a fucked up bunch, aren't we."

"Indeed. Heroes in old stories aren't all bruised and beaten up, are they?" Zero asked.

"Not usually, but then it might just be the author leaving out those details. They are stories after all."

"Still, I hope we get our nice heroic ending, with everyone cheering for us," Zero said. "I'm at least hoping to not get kicked out of the guard for this."

"I bet there's going to be a meeting and discussions." Ivy sighed. "I fucking hate that."

"It'll be worth it to get rid of those things, though," Calla said.

"Indeed," Zero said. "Well, my lovely and brave crew, let's get going."

Calla didn't feel especially lovely or brave at the moment. She felt exhausted and wary of what was to come. Powder wasn't used all that often in the area; she knew further south they used it to blow into the mountains to mine for iron and other things, and during war it was used to blast into castles and such, but around here, there wasn't much use for it.

They only had it and briefly trained with it because all guards did. Now they were going to go underground and try to block a cavern by blowing part of it up. There was a not-so-small chance that they were going to end up burying themselves in the process. Calla could only hope in that instance that it was quick; she'd rather be crushed to death than be trapped in the darkness, waiting to die from lack of air or water.

"I know you're worried, Calla, and probably mostly for good reason, but remember, I do have a decent amount of experience with powder," Zero said with a smile.

"Do we even want to know?" Ivy asked.

"I grew up near a place that made powder. They'd pay good coin to young boys willing to test it," Zero said.

"Good that someone had experience with it," Calla said. "I don't remember how to use it. I'm not really good at anything."

"You are," Ivy said.

"I don't know about that," Calla said. She didn't really see herself as that, though she had done things in the past few days that she wouldn't have guessed she could possibly do. She was nervous the whole time, but she had done it and she was still there and still willing to push forward.

"I do," Zero said. "You are a phenomenal guard, Calla."

"Thank you," she said.

"Aww, you made her blush," Ivy said.

"Shut up, Ivy," Calla said. "I ... I believe you, Zero, I don't think I would have a few days ago, but now I do. And you are doing a fantastic job as well."

"Thank you."

"Ah yes, making each other feel good before we go to blow ourselves up in a cave," Ivy said.

Calla snorted a laugh and Zero chuckled.

"We're going to try to avoid dying as much as possible," he said.

"Of course," Ivy said.

"I'd rather not."

"But ... " Zero hesitated. "It might happen. I think we all know that."

"Yeah," Ivy said, and Calla nodded. She had no idea, really, what to expect. She wanted it to go like in a story where they would easily defeat their foes and come back victorious to a cheering crowd, but that wasn't really likely to happen, was it?

Three wounded, tired guards trying to do something nearly impossible. Surely something would go wrong. But she supposed things had been going wrong for a while now, and they just had to work with what they had and fight until they couldn't fight anymore.

The cave opening was clear of any creatures, and the cave itself was empty. Not a whiff of rotting apple or blood. If Calla didn't know better, she would say that the whole thing had been a dream, or a nightmare, really.

They walked through the cave as quickly as they could. Calla was surprised how much she remembered about the way even though she had only been there once.

"I see the light," Zero said. "That's insane."

"We need to be careful," Calla said. "With the sun behind us, there might be a shadow and enough darkness for the creatures to come out."

"I hope they're asleep, mostly because I want to surprise the fuck out of them," Ivy said.

"So far, so good," Zero said. "I can see why you don't want to blow this, Ivy."

"Has to be done, I'll figure something out," Ivy said. "Right now I just want it done, and I want to go back to the fort and nap for days."

"Time to play with powder." Zero smiled. "If you two would kindly keep a lookout."

"Yes, sir," Calla said. Ivy moved away from where Zero was setting up the powder bombs to look at the forest. Calla followed her over and looked at the strange landscape beyond.

"I want to know what's out there, but then again, I don't. I have a feeling I could find ten things that would kill a person just walking a few feet in." Ivy paced back and forth a bit, looking at all the plants.

"Most likely," Calla said. It was beautiful, though, and so different from anything she had ever seen, but she could imagine how many of those things would be crawling around the forest at night.

"I will find a way back out here," Ivy said.

"I know you can do it," Calla said. She turned around to look at Zero to see how he was doing and found that he was looking between the two of them. He gave her a thumbs-up and Calla blushed and turned away.

Two birds with odd-looking black and white feathers cried out and flew from a nearby tree.

"Fuck," Ivy said, and Calla looked over and saw two of the creatures coming out of one of the holes in the ground. It was still a little light out, but they were clinging to the shadows. So far, it didn't look like Ivy and Calla had been spotted, but it was only a matter of time.

Calla drew her sword as quietly as she could and Ivy did the same, and as they were doing so, three more creatures came out. Ivy took a few steps back toward Calla, and they both moved so they could be in between Zero and the creatures.

Calla turned to Zero, who was busy setting up the charges and seemed unaware of what was going on. Calla debated whether or not to try to get his attention; she could cause the creatures to notice them, but then again, if Zero started talking loudly without realizing it, they would attack anyway.

Luckily Zero looked up and saw Calla and Ivy then looked beyond them to the creatures. He stared at them for just a moment then went back to furiously setting up the charges.

Calla thought they were in a good position to ...

It only took an instant for the creatures to notice them and start an attack. They started hissing and stalking, and more creatures came out of the crack. But they didn't seem eager to attack as fast as they normally did.

"What are they doing?" Ivy asked.

"I don't know, maybe they get more defensive of their home?" Calla said. She started looking around in case there was somewhere else they were crawling out of or sneaking up on them from, but she couldn't see anything.

"Alright," Zero said not long after. "Ready to go."

Calla and Ivy moved back slowly. If they ran, the creatures would probably chase them, though every bone in Calla's body was telling her to run. A few of the creatures started to follow them as they retreated into the cave.

Calla hoped that none of the creatures would follow them back, but they could manage to take one or two of them out if they were left in the tunnel after the explosion.

"I'm going to light this, and then we'll run back a bit further. Once it goes, cover your heads. As messed up as it sounds, it's better to have a broken arm than a cracked skull," Zero said.

"Lovely thought," Ivy said.

"Ready?"

Zero lit the fuse, and they all ran back down the tunnel to where they thought would be a safe enough distance.

At least three of the creatures came after them, but something about the smell of the lit fuse made them stop, luckily just under where the explosion would be.

The powder went off, sending a near-deafening sound of rocks cascading down.

"That sounded about right," Zero said. "We should … "

The world dropped out from under them, and the sound of cascading rocks once again filled the air. The tunnel was collapsing, Calla realized. There must be something under them, another cavern that they were falling into.

They were doomed. There was no way they would survive. They would be crushed for certain. Calla tried to reach out for Ivy but couldn't find her. Her last thought before they hit the bottom was hope that at the very least, the creatures would be blocked, and they would not have died in vain.

8

———

IN THE DARK

Ivy could make out a little light; at least one of the torches or lanterns was still burning in the darkness of the cave. Everything was silent aside from her own breathing. Fuck. Was everyone else dead? Ivy knew she was very much alive because she was in pain, but she didn't really want to have to focus on how badly she was hurt. She didn't want to move, she really didn't, but it didn't sound like anyone else was alive, and she had to know.

"Fuck it," she said and moved her arms. Good there. She felt her head, and there was something sticky, blood, obviously, on the side of her forehead, but it wasn't enough to be concerned about. She felt her chest and stomach, and nothing felt too bad, sore, but not bad.

She moved her right leg. Fine. Left …

"Oh fuck, fuck damn it fuck!" Well, at least it was the same leg as the twisted ankle. Something in her lower leg was broken.

"Calla! Zero!" she called out and listened. Nothing. She couldn't even hear anyone breathing nearby.

"Fuck! Please, I don't want to be alone ... "

Light. There was still light. She could find the still-burning torch and try to find Calla and Zero ... at least find their bodies. She had to try to get out for them. So someone would know what happened.

Ivy half-stumbled, half-crawled to the light of the torch. She stopped just before she got to it with a gasp.

Calla.

She was lying on her stomach, very still. Ivy took a deep breath before reaching for the torch. She moved some of Calla's dark hair aside and felt for a pulse at her neck, expecting to find nothing.

But there was something. A pulse, and a strong one at that.

"Calla?" Ivy moved around to the other side of Calla so she could see better. "Calla, honey, please wake up."

Calla groaned and Ivy looked over her body for any injuries. She had a nasty gash on her upper left arm, a cut across her cheek. Ivy carefully felt Calla's head and couldn't find any broken skin or bone.

"Ivy?"

"Calla! Oh thank the spirits, where are you hurt, honey?"

"Honey. I like it," Calla said. She moved slowly, and when she turned onto her back, she grunted.

"Calla?"

"Ribs," Calla said, holding her hand over her lower left ribs.

"Can I take a look?" Ivy asked, and Calla nodded. Calla's skin was bruised, swollen, and hot, and the ribs felt odd, probably broken. But the bruising didn't look too bad or so Ivy hoped.

"Where is Zero?" Calla asked.

"I haven't found him yet," Ivy said. "I'll try to, but my leg's fucked." Ivy saw a flash of light and blinked as Zero came into view.

"Zero?"

Zero let out a long sigh. "Thank goodness. Fuck, I couldn't do it again."

"Come here. How bad are you hurt?" Ivy asked.

"Broke a couple ribs for sure," Zero said. "Bloody and bruised. How are you two?"

"My leg is broken," Ivy said.

"Broken ribs," Calla said.

"We're still alive and still have light," Zero said. "We're going to try to get home as best we can. All of us."

"Yes, sir," Calla said softly.

"I'm not fucking done yet," Ivy said. She really didn't want to think about moving in her condition and trying to climb out and crawl through rocks with a broken fucking leg, but she really didn't want to die down in the cavern, and she didn't want Calla or Zero to either.

"Let's take stock of what we have and look around a bit. Gather our wits," Zero said.

One of the lanterns was still in working order, and once they found the wood from the other torches, they each had a light. Ivy closed her eyes and took some deep breaths. She was facing east. She could feel it, just as she had always felt it. There was no way out east; it was all blocked, which likely indicated that they had successfully closed the gap. Well, they would find out soon enough. If there were creatures and they could get through, they would undoubtedly come after wounded prey.

The tunnel they should have taken to get out ran west, and that direction looked passable. She told Zero and Calla as much.

Calla was searching nearby for their packs or anything useful. What they really needed was something to brace Ivy's leg with so it didn't break worse. She wondered if she was going to lose the leg. Fuck. *Don't think about it, not now.*

Ivy tried to focus on something else, and something made her focus in on Zero's breathing. She could hear his breaths hitch in pain, and it sounded like he couldn't take a deep breath. She lifted her torch slightly.

"Zero? How bad is it?"

He looked for a moment like he was about to deny anything being wrong, but he let out a shaky sigh. "Not good. I think a rib might have punctured my lung, it really hurts to breathe and it's hard to get a good breath."

"We should try to get going, then," Ivy said. "If you think you can."

"I can," Zero said.

"I found my pack," Calla said. "Most of what was in it was crushed, but I think we can use it and the straps to brace Ivy's leg a little."

"Sounds like fun," Ivy said.

Ivy cried out in pain as Calla worked on bracing her leg. Lightning bolts of pain ran down to her toes and then all the way up into her lower back. It felt like a million fire ants were in her leg, and she was half-tempted to take her sword and cut the fucking thing off.

By the time Calla was done, Ivy was shaking and tears were streaming down her face. Fuck, she didn't know how she was going to manage to get out of the damn cave.

"I'm sorry," Calla said.

"Had to do it," Ivy managed. "We should get moving." It was the last thing she wanted to do, but Zero was badly hurt and they needed to get him to Ramona at the fort so she could patch him up. They couldn't delay.

Ivy felt a little dizzy as she stood and tried to fight down the pain. The path before them was strewn with boulders and loose rocks, but it did lead in the right direction and in a vaguely upward trajectory.

It was a struggle. Every single step was a struggle. They were all moaning and groaning as they moved, trying to pick the best path through. They couldn't see where they were going. For all they knew, there would be nothing but a dead end at the top.

Ivy tried the best she could to move on her own. She had a feeling that Zero was going to need to be helped before long, and if Calla was helping her, it would be hard for her to leave Ivy to help Zero.

Zero was really starting to struggle. He was panting for air and groaning in pain. Every time Ivy glanced over at him, Zero looked like he was about to fall over. But he kept pushing forward.

Calla was doing well. She was being careful and holding her left side where her wounded ribs were, but she wasn't making as much of a fuss as Ivy and Zero were. She would make it out for certain. She was a lot tougher than she looked. Ivy thought she would make it as well. She was very concerned about her leg, but she'd pull through.

Ivy wasn't sure about Zero.

Ivy tried to focus on the path ahead; they were finally nearing the top of what they could see. It felt right, like they could be just below where the usual path went, and they would pop up into the main tunnel and be able to stumble out into the light.

Calla made it to the top first and rested against a boulder and tried to catch her breath. She was quiet and didn't say anything, and it had Ivy worried. Then Calla lifted the torch and looked around.

"I think we're back up into the main tunnel," Calla said. Ivy pushed herself forward through the pain. She had to see it. She finally got to where Calla was and looked at the tunnel ahead.

It was the same tunnel. They made it. They would be able to walk out after all. Calla and Ivy stepped onto the main path. Zero came up behind them, stumbling forward and leaning heavily against the wall of the cave.

With a groan, Zero slid down the wall and started to cough. "Zero? Fuck."

"I can't breathe ... " Zero groaned again.

"Just rest a minute, Zero. You said we're all getting out of here and we are," Calla said.

Zero nodded. Calla looked at Ivy, her brow furrowed and lips pursed. Ivy shrugged. It looked bad, but they were all pushing themselves hard.

"I'm going to scout ahead a little, make sure it's safe," Calla said. "You two rest."

Ivy was glad for a little break and even managed to find a position where she could rest more comfortably. Even Zero's breathing evened out a bit. It was still labored and rough, and Ivy really didn't like the sound of it.

"We'll get you out, Zero, we'll get you out into the light again. I know you can make it that far," Ivy said.

Zero nodded. "I think I can, but I don't ... I don't know ... "

"Just focus on the first part, getting out. Calla and I won't abandon you," Ivy said. She shifted slightly so their shoulders were touching, and she reached out and took Zero's hand. Calla came back and looked between the two, and Ivy could see fear in her eyes, not for the tunnel, she was sure, but for Zero.

"It looks good ahead," Calla said. Her gaze lingered on Zero, and she looked for a moment like she was going to say something but didn't.

"Good, let's get the fuck out of here," Ivy said. She managed to get up and managed to help Calla get Zero up. He groaned in pain, and as they moved on, he continued to cry out every so often from the pain. It was hard to support him; he had incurred so many wounds over the past few days.

They really didn't have far to go, but they had to move so slowly with how badly they were all hurt. There were times when Ivy thought that Zero was going to fall over. She didn't know, really didn't know, if they would be able to get him back to the fort.

She wondered how quickly Calla could run down to get Ramona and bring her back, if there would be enough time to do so before Zero succumbed to his injuries. One thing was certain, she was not going to leave Zero alone to … die.

Ivy didn't want to think that way, but things didn't look good. All they could do was try their best, and at the very least, Zero wouldn't be alone. When she first woke up, she had been terrified of the thought of being alone. Zero wouldn't have to worry about that.

"I see light ahead," Calla exclaimed. Ivy saw it too, and hopefully Zero did as well. They were almost out.

"Almost there, Zero," Ivy said.

Once they got out into the light, they would have to rest. Ivy's leg was throbbing and she felt like she could fall over at any moment, and Zero needed to rest again. They needed to have a realistic conversation about what Zero wanted to do next.

All three of them managed to stumble out of the cave and into the early morning light. Ivy was just helping Zero sit down, and also trying to sit down herself, when she heard a noise.

"There they are," someone said. "Arrest them."

***

Calla glared at the man and looked back at Zero and Ivy, who were both absolutely worn out, and Zero really didn't look good.

"No!" Calla said. "There will be no arrests until we receive medical attention. That is the most pressing matter, sir."

"Who are you?"

"I am Calla. I have served at the Caldera for over twenty years. Due to the recent incident, Zero was temporary leader, and he made me his second in case of further emergency. There is a lot to be dealt with and handled, but first and foremost, we are all hurt, and Zero especially bad. Medical attention needs to be the priority, sir," Calla said.

The captain looked at her then over her shoulder at Zero and Ivy.

"You are quite right, forgive me. Medic!"

Calla breathed a sigh of relief. She was still shaking a little as she walked back to Ivy and Zero and as Ramona came from behind the captain and headed straight to Zero.

"Holding on, Ivy?" Ramona asked.

"I'll be fine, leg's just fucked," Ivy said. "Again."

Calla sat down opposite Zero and took his hand as Ramona began looking him over.

"That was awesome, Calla," Zero said. "I knew you had it in you."

"Thank you, Zero." Calla smiled. Now that they were out into the light, now that they were not fighting to survive, now that it was done, it was clear how badly hurt Zero was. He was breathing fast even though he was lying down. He was far too pale.

Ramona was listening to Zero's chest with a frown on her face. Calla still had a little hope that maybe, just maybe, they could help Zero pull out of this. Ramona lifted Zero's shirt, and Calla saw the bruising and her stomach twisted. Ramona put her hand on Zero's chest and then his stomach, and Zero let out a groan of pain.

"His lung's collapsed," Ramona said. "Broken ribs, internal bleeding."

"Dying?" Zero asked.

"Not just yet. I can put a tube in your chest to get rid of the air and blood. I don't know if I can stop the bleeding, but I can try. There is a chance you'll pull through."

Zero closed his eyes and let out a groan. Calla squeezed his hand.

"You can tell me to stop whenever you want, Zero, and I'll respect that," Ramona said. Ivy moved closer to them and put a hand on Zero's shoulder.

"We're with you no matter what," Ivy said.

Zero looked at them then focused on Ramona. "I'll try."

"Alright, Ivy and Calla, if you could each keep hold of one of his arms, be ready to hold him down a bit. We'll get the tube in and see if he stabilizes."

Ramona worked quickly; it seemed only a matter of moments between her rummaging in her bag and being ready for the procedure.

"Alright, Zero," Ramona said. "I'm sorry, this is going to hurt."

"Do it," Zero said. Zero cried out in pain and squeezed Calla's hand hard. There was a horrible gurgling, hissing noise as blood and air came out of the tube in Zero's chest. It looked horrible, and Calla looked at Ramona to see if it was as bad as it looked.

"That's it, Zero, just breathe," Ramona said. Zero did. His breathing hitched in pain and he still looked far too pale, but he was hanging on. Zero kept breathing, and after a few minutes, it even seemed like he was taking deeper breaths.

"Easier to breathe?" Ramona asked.

"Yes, still hurts," Zero said.

"I know, I'll get to that," Ramona said. The next few minutes were spent listening to Zero breathe and Ramona checking Zero's vitals. It didn't look like he was getting better, but it didn't look like he was getting worse either.

"Alright," Ramona said. "I think he's stable enough to move down to the fort. We'll take it slow and have to take breaks, probably, but I think we can move."

"I can do it," Zero said. His voice was shaky and weak, but there was a look of determination in his eyes that Calla thought was a good sign. They had to make two stretchers, one for Zero and one for Ivy, even though she told them to fuck off at first.

"Stay with Zero," Ivy said. "He needs it more right now."

"I'll see you at the fort," Calla said. Calla was a bit too short to carry Zero, but she held his hand the whole way down to the fort. He moaned in pain often, but he kept breathing and managed to stay awake.

"You're doing well, Zero, getting closer," Calla squeezed his hand and he squeezed back. Calla had never been happier to see the fort. She knew that there was still going to be a struggle to keep Zero alive, but it felt like it would be easier at the fort.

Calla followed Zero and Ivy to the healing room.

"Still holding on, Zero?" Ramona asked as she checked his pulse and listened to his chest.

"Still here," Zero said.

"Good. Calla, can you help me with Ivy?"

"Do we have to do this?" Ivy asked.

"You know we do. It's not going to take that much manipulation, it'll be quick," Ramona said. "It's a simple break, should heal cleanly."

"Fine," Ivy said and held tight to Calla's hand.

"You'll be alright," Calla said. Ramona got ready and Ivy groaned in anticipation.

"Ahhhh, fuck shit damn it all to hell motherfucking fuck!" Ivy yelled. Calla tried hard not to laugh at Ivy's profanity. Ramona wrapped the leg up quickly, and Ivy's breathing calmed down.

"That's it, Ivy, we're done, I'll get you something for the pain," Ramona said.

"Ugh, that sucked."

"I'm sorry," Calla said.

"How's Zero?" Ivy asked.

"Hanging in there," Ramona said. "His pulse is stable, and he's breathing well enough now. I don't think he's losing too much blood. It'll be touch and go for a few days, healing might take some time, but I'm hopeful. Right, Calla, let's take a look at your ribs."

The next few days were a blur for Calla. She spent most of her time in the infirmary looking after Ivy and Zero. Ivy was alright; she was mostly just bored and needed company.

Zero ... Ramona wasn't lying when she said it would be touch and go. He was unconscious most of the time, and his breathing sounded rough and painful. There were times when it was quiet in the night that it sounded like Zero might stop breathing.

When Ivy was asleep, Calla would spend some time holding Zero's hand and putting a cool cloth on his forehead to help with the fever.

It was rough for a few days.

The captain, Campion was his name, luckily was a patient man and wasn't insisting on talking to Ivy and Calla just yet. Maybe he was waiting to see if Zero pulled through before he decided what to do.

9

A NEW NORMAL

Calla and Ivy made their way to meet with Captain Campion. They had been back a couple of days, and so far everything was going well. There were no signs of the creatures, and Zero was recovering well.

Calla was a little nervous about why Campion wanted to talk just to her and Ivy, though. Surely he didn't think Zero was at fault for anything?

"We started off on the wrong foot, I apologize for that. There is a lot going on with this situation, and we are both partially in the dark. For one, the only reason I was in Hennan was because I was on my way to replace Captain Marcus."

"I didn't know that," Calla said.

Campion nodded. "I doubt he would have told anyone. Now, Lieutenant Zero had an incident in the past ... "

"I am aware of it," Calla said.

" ... Marcus was always of the opinion that Zero slipped out of any repercussions. Marcus may have been looking for a way to keep his position by bringing who he assumed was a criminal to justice."

"Ah, that would make sense," Calla said.

"It also seems like Asher didn't quite like Zero, or Ivy, for that matter."

"I'm well aware of that," Ivy said.

"I believe he was in shock as well. This was a situation none of us could have foreseen," Calla said.

"Tell me what happened here," Campion said.

Calla and Ivy told him in as much detail as they could the events of the few days when the creatures were attacking. It was hard to believe so much had happened in a few days when usually so little happened in a year.

Calla made sure to stick as close to the facts as she could. She didn't think anyone was really to blame, not even Marcus, and the man was not there to defend himself. Asher had been dealing with the shock of the situation. She did make sure that she mentioned all of what Zero had done. He had risked his life and almost died, and she wasn't going to let his name get dragged through the mud, and she was going to try to make sure he stayed in the guard.

Campion nodded when she was done, and for a while, they sat in silence. Then Campion spoke. "Now, there is a lot of cleanup and restructuring and rebuilding to do. You used quite a lot of wood in defending the fort, and winter is almost here. It's going to be a long hard winter here, and we can only keep a small squad. I would like you two to stay since you know the area well."

"I will stay, sir. I've been here all of my career and would like to help," Calla said. "As long as Lieutenant Zero remains here as well."

Campion smiled. "I thought you might say that. Yes, Zero is staying, if he wants to, that is. And I'll be training him to take over this fort. He'll need some help, of course, so

congratulations, lieutenants, I feel I'll be relying on you two a lot this winter."

"Thank you, sir," Calla said.

"Thank you, sir," Ivy echoed.

Campion smiled and left Calla in a daze. Lieutenant. She had been promoted. Less than a week ago, she was too scared to talk to Captain Marcus and now she had a promotion. Life was very weird sometimes.

"We're fucking lieutenants, what the hell," Ivy said, breaking Calla out of her mind.

"That's not really how I saw this going, to be honest," Calla said.

Calla and Ivy waited for Campion to get done talking to Zero before coming into his room to see what he had decided.

"I'm surprised you two waited until Campion was gone," Zero said.

"Barely," Ivy said. "So, are you staying? Future captain?"

"With you two as my lieutenants? Of course I'm staying. And I don't feel like having to move with these damn ribs," Zero said.

"So, what's the plan, captain?" Ivy asked.

"Survive winter, heal," Zero said.

"And ... plan to find a way into the Caldera?"

"As long as it doesn't involve me," Zero said. "It would be good to make sure we're safe, and if you can get in without those things getting out, that's fine by me."

"Yes!" Ivy said. Zero laughed a little bit then wrapped his hand around his ribs and winced.

"You alright, Calla?" Zero asked.

"Yes, better than that. Just I still can't believe all this happened," she said. "We almost lost you."

Zero smiled. "I'm still here."

"That was rough," Ivy said.

"I knew you cared." Zero smirked.

"Oh shut up," Ivy said, and they all laughed.

***

Ivy tried to be as quiet as she could, but it wasn't fucking easy on crutches. She didn't want to wake Calla just yet. Normally on such a cold winter day, she would want to stay in bed with Calla as much as possible, but she needed to look outside. She was absolutely sure it had snowed, and quite a bit, overnight.

The air just had a certain feeling to it. There was just something different about the first snow of the season. By the end of winter, Ivy knew she would be sick to shit of looking out at all the white, but the first snow? That was something to celebrate.

She opened their door slightly and saw at least six inches of snow. Well, fuck, it was going to be harder to hobble around with it, but it was still so pretty. The air was nippy, the fort in near silence as snow still fell.

It was beautiful.

"It snowed?"

Ivy jumped a little and turned to see Calla, who was almost doubled over laughing.

"Fuck off," Ivy said.

"Sorry, sorry," Calla said. "I'll get us some breakfast. You'll end up in the snow if you try to walk through this before we clear a path."

"Probably. Thanks, honey," Ivy said. Calla smiled and blushed, and it was so cute that Ivy had to pull Calla in for a kiss.

Ivy watched Calla pick her way through the snow and smiled. Winter was a hard season, but it was nice to have someone to go through it with for a change. It was nice to have someone around for everything for a change.

Ivy was standing and watching when suddenly a snowball hit her in the shoulder and she heard laughing. She saw Zero peeking out of his doorway.

"Oh, you are dead," Ivy said.

"No no no wait, mercy, I'm still healing!"

"So am I!" Ivy said and made sure to aim high enough to miss Zero's chest and hit him square in the face.

"Ugh, insubordination! Lashes for you!" Zero cried dramatically. Ivy was sure that if he were fully healed, he would flop down in the snow and pretend to be dead.

"Could you two stop trying to kill each other? Breakfast is ready," Calla said.

"Thank you, Calla," Zero said.

"Thanks, babe," Ivy said. "We're coming over to bug you, Captain."

The three sat down and dug into the oatmeal. It was oatmeal yesterday and it would be oatmeal for the rest of the winter. It was like that every winter, though. Looking around at her girlfriend and friend, Ivy wouldn't change anything.

ACKNOWLEDGEMENTS

Thank you to my family for always being supportive.

ABOUT THE AUTHOR

A. E. has been writing since she was fourteen and has always had an interest in the whump genre.

— · —

BEFORE YOU GO

This is the fifth book in 12 Months of Whump, a series of whumpy novellas published by WPP throughout 2025. Each novella can be read as a standalone.
To stay up to date with the 12 Months of Whump series and other whumperfly-inducing projects, visit us at
https://thewhumpyprintingpress.tumblr.com/

www.ingramcontent.com/pod-product-compliance
Lightning Source LLC
Chambersburg PA
CBHW052007170626
46808CB00007B/2810